Mystery House

Kurt Steel

MURDER IS A FACT

Mystery House

MURDER IS A FACT

For more titles in the Mystery House library,
visit our website: **www.FictionHousePress.com**

"Murder is a Fact" was published as a 4-part serial in *Scribner's Magazine* for May to August 1938. Copyright 1938 by Harlan Logan Associates Inc.

isbn 978-1-64720-412-9

First Mystery House edition August 2021

FICTION HOUSE PRESS
www.FictionHousePress.com

I

THE OFFICES of the national weekly, *Fact*, were pubicized by *Fact's* alert young ideagenic (the word was their own) promotion staff as "the nerve center of immediate history."

One day out of every week—Tuesday—even a dull visitor must have sensed the modest rightness of the phrase. Tuesday was closing day for Friday's issue. On Tuesday *Fact's* waiting room, where murals of men and machines and ships and grain splashed from wall to wall, pulsed with a special tension. Men came and went through the room, their words quick, phrases hastily clipped. Those who waited in chromium chairs below the flaring murals caught, one by one, the signal of a sharp-faced boy at the reception desk and rose to plunge through a wide, studded door.

When the door swung open it disclosed a long corridor leading to a distant light-filled room where typewriters clattered, automatic printers spread their barrage of monotonous clacking, doors in glass partitions slammed, bells rang, the mingled

1

clamor overflowing and washing back and forth in the corridor like flood tide in a lagoon.

It was the not undocumented boast of *Fact's* editorial staff that on Tuesdays, when Friday's issue was going to bed, they hurtled through the work of seven metropolitan city rooms under a pressure no city editor could have stood for three hours. Only the digits in this boast were ever protested by newspapermen.

On a certain Tuesday in August, while the tumult was at its midafternoon peak, Baird Henderson, tall, angular, chief of *Fact's* editorial staff, stepped into the corridor from a door bearing his name. He carried a sheaf of paper, and as he strode along, his sharp cynical eyes scanned the top page. Henderson's long asymmetrical face was fatigued, but through the fatigue there showed a mordant amusement, traces of which were rarely absent for long from his mouth, his casually observant gray eyes.

A door opened, and Henderson collided with *Fact's* slighter, compact, intense editor, Hugh Flint. An expression of nervous annoyance leaped into Flint's sharply angled face.

Henderson said, "I was looking for you."

"What is it, Baird?" Flint's tone was sharp.

Henderson held out the papers. He rubbed one cheek and his mouth slanted. "Dynamite."

A messenger carrying a locked pouch ran past them. A boy came up, said, "Mr. Flint," urgently. Flint, his sharp, nervous eyes on the page Henderson had given him, ignored the boy who waited respectfully.

At thirty-eight Hugh Flint, vice-president of the corporation he had envisaged while still a Harvard undergraduate, had already achieved a success which might have baffled a lesser man. Son of a watchman in the Whitford Cotton Works, he had as a youth impressed the elderly childless Cornelius Whitford and been made that tycoon's protege. At Harvard, where Whitford sent him, his driving genius had propelled him into high undergraduate political places and fused an alliance with Philip Norton, whose social and financial connections were exactly what Flint needed in order to realize his one burning ambition—the establishment of a magazine whose power would be as the power of any ten of its predecessors. Between them Flint and Norton had founded Fact, Incorporated, staffed it with Harvard colleagues of their college days, and brilliantly had guided *Fact* to its destiny. No member of the organization, with the exception of Flint and Norton, was ever mentioned by name, and thus on these two was indivisibly focused the brilliance of *Fact's* reputation—on Flint, fiery originator, and Norton, *Fact's* sapient business director.

Baird Henderson, classmate of Flint's and Norton's at Harvard, quiet dependable third of a trinity that had made Yard history, had at the inception of *Fact* been entrusted with the detailed carrying out of Flint's meteoric ideas, and was by now as indispensable in the vivid life of the organization as Flint himself—a fact on which Henderson, troubled with neither Norton's financial ambitions nor Flint's lust for power, had never considered it worth while to insist. Save for rare periods of introspective revolt,

Henderson was content to enjoy the anonymity which Flint's and Norton's combined shadow gave him. When rebellion did warm him on occasion he was wont to turn the mild acid of his amusement on the flickering spark and extinguish it.

Which was exactly what he was doing now as he waited for Flint to finish reading the copy he had handed him.

Copyboys, more messengers, young men in eye-shades hurried by. Henderson did not take his ironic eyes off Flint. "Just a little libel in it, Hugh?"

Flint answered shortly without looking up. "The facts always libel someone. That's why they're facts." He thrust the sheets at Henderson. "Time to remake 'Personalities' to take this?"

Henderson looked at his watch. "Twenty-seven minutes."

"Fine," Flint snapped, his unquiet eyes bright. "Remake 'Personalities' and give this Danisher business two columns."

"Why not send a man out with a gun to shoot Danisher? Simpler that way."

Flint frowned sharply and strode away. Henderson watched him a moment, glanced at the typed pages in his hand, drew his mouth down, and returned to his own office.

A moment later there was a rap on the panel. Henderson said, "Come in."

The boy who had waited respectfully for Flint to finish reading as he stood in the corridor entered. "Mr. Flint wants you, Mr. Henderson. He's in the cable room."

Halfway down the corridor, Henderson entered a

square room where a dozen telegraphers sat in cubicles, each with a depleted roll of manifold feeding into his typewriter like the web of newsprint into a press. Several of the keys were still clicking, but their tempo was relaxed. The wires, each leading to one of the earth's current hotspots, would be held open until the last form was plated up, but it was clear that the flood had already receded from this outpost.

Flint was leaning over the shoulder of one operator whose fingers were translating a dispatch into type. "Jake," he said crisply as Henderson approached, "get a confirmation on that Tokyo riot. We'll try to hold for it."

The man hitched his quadruplicate sheets nervously, leaning forward with weary fingers to adjust the roll from which they unwound. His key leaped into life.

Flint turned, saw Henderson, and motioned him to the door. Outside, he said frowning, "Baird, Danisher is out front. I'm sending out word to have him talk to you."

Henderson stared at the other, one mobile eyebrow lifting. "Thanks."

"You're not afraid of him?" Flint challenged.

"Why?"

"Will you talk to him?"

Henderson shook his head.

"Why not?" Flint barked.

Henderson said, "Scenes are bad for my nerves. Send him in to see Phil," he suggested.

Flint's eyes narrowed. He said, "All right. Tell Mac," and walked rapidly away.

Henderson stood a moment, his eyebrow still lifted. Then, hearing his name called, he turned toward the wide noisy room at the end of the corridor where the Production Manager was signaling him. Along the far wall a battery of clacking automatic printers made endless din. Operators worked tensely at keyboards, punching tape that writhed into the clattering senders. Boys trotted along, snaring sheaves of last-minute revisions on spindles—last-minute revisions that would beat Sunday editions of every newspaper in the country. Behind a triple-glass wall a score of youths with earphones and breastplates sat poised over copy that had been sent through the machines thirty minutes before and was even now being read back in proof over a thousand miles of telephone cable from the humming production and distribution plant in the Middle West, where forms were being tightened and presses were already pounding out the back pages of the weekly run.

II

HENDERSON, returning by way of the quieter, depopulated art room, encountered Philip Norton talking to the Art Editor. He told Norton that Flint had suggested Norton see Danisher. "Pleasant little prospect," he added.

Norton frowned. The frown, like everything else about his erect, athletic person, was faultless; it lent gravity to the smooth pinkness of his face, touched rounded jowl and the cleft of his chin with a passing austerity. A perfectly controlled frown, a frown unquestionably in leash, efficient, amenable, like all Norton's gestures, to the exigencies of time and place. The frown vanished.

"Thank you, Baird. I'd like for you to be there too, if you will," suavely.

Henderson's mouth twisted.

"You arranged the research and know more about what we have found out than I do, you know."

"I'll come in." Henderson walked away.

"Thank you, Baird." Norton turned to the Art

Editor and continued his calm discussion. When he had finished, he went to his paneled office where the financial policy of *Fact* was shaped.

Here he was met by a wiry youth with slate-colored eyes sharpened by octagonal, rimless glasses.

When Hugh Flint had, the spring before, announced his intention of adapting to journalism a device hitherto monopolized by football coaches and Hollywood studios, he had aroused amusement in the publication world and thrown a hundred college campuses into ferment. In short, Flint stated that henceforth *Fact* would scout the colleges for journalistic talent, signing promising upperclassmen to write for the magazine after their graduation. The harshness of the criteria by which such *enfants terribles* were to be selected, however, was manifest at once. Only one was chosen the first June.

His name was Clark Malory, and his admiration for Flint was of the order of pure hero worship. Malory had exhibited this in his sophomore year by dragooning a dozen of his fellows into an organization patterned on Fact, Incorporated, and by publishing at his family's expense a collegiate weekly which followed its professional model so closely as to be accused by some captious critics of plagiarism. The sprightly tone of the publication, its success in producing two journalistic beats which metropolitan dailies were honest enough to recognize as such, and above all Malory's reiterated and passionate admiration for the Editor-in-Chief of *Fact*, all brought him to Flint's attention, and to the informed it was matter for no surprise when Clark

Malory was announced as the recipient of the first *Fact* contract to be awarded an undergraduate anywhere in the nation. *College Humor* carried an encomium, Clark's coterie began referring to him as The Future Editor of *Fact*, and Clark wore his mouth differently.

During this summer he was being inducted into the close fraternity of the *Fact* staff, and was currently serving as Norton's assistant while the regular incumbent took his vacation.

Now something in the youth's manner made Norton frown. He asked, "What is it, Clark?"

The Future Editor of *Fact* said in a terse editorial manner, "Trouble, Mr. Norton."

"What kind of trouble?"

Polished highlights on the rimless glasses sharpened. "Danisher is here."

Norton's frown vanished. His round, pink face was imperturable, competent. He nodded.

"Shall I have Mr. Flint talk to him?"

The merest echo of Norton's frown flitted over his calm eyes. "Do you think he could do it better than I?"

Clark flushed. He said, "I'll have Danisher come in."

Norton glanced at his watch. "Call Henderson. Tell Danisher he can have three minutes, no more."

A minute later he rose from behind his desk as the door opened and a tall, spare man with angular jaw and jutting chin was ushered in. Clark Malory looked after him for an instant, his youthful eyes hard, his cheeks still flushed. Then he closed the door, and Banisher and Norton were alone for a moment.

"Mr. Danisher?" Norton asked cordially.

"I am." Danisher's eyes, deep beneath their furze of brow, glittered. "I hear that you arc planning to print——"

The corridor door opened, and Baird Henderson strode into the room. He looked sharply from Norton to the stranger.

"This is Mr. Danisher, Mr. Henderson," Norton said smoothly. "Won't you sit down, Mr. Danisher?"

"I want to know if it's true that you are going to print a story about my face lotion containing—"

"Mr. Henderson," the Production Manager cried, rushing through the door which Henderson still held open, "Johnson's come in with a double spread for Black and Black. How in God's name we going to——?"

"What can you cut?" Norton asked Henderson.

Henderson rubbed his cheek, his bloodshot eyes on his watch. The tumult in the corridor quickened moment by moment, eddied into the room like the lapping waves of a flood at crest.

"Youth movement story," Henderson rapped out. "Sent it through five minutes ago and——"

A boy skidded through the door and thrust a sheaf of soiled dummies into the Production Manager's hand.

"Do sit down, Mr. Danisher," Norton urged.

"My God," the Production Manager wailed, looking up wildly from the sheets in his hand. "Twenty-four's been plated up for two days. What's this tripe from Buenos Aires doing in——?"

"We are printing a report from the laboratory

which——" Norton began to Danisher.

"I should like to see that report, Mr. Norton."

"I'm sorry, Danisher, but——"

"*What* did you say to do with this Buenos Aires——?"

"Replate page twenty-four," Henderson snapped.

The Production Manager's drawn face sagged. He murmured something and wheeled to charge out of the room and upset a messenger boy. The door closed slowly, muting the clamor that swelled ever higher.

"That report," Norton said easily, almost genially, to Danisher, "indicates that every woman who uses your cosmetics runs the risk of paralysis or death, Danisher."

"*Not* every woman," the manufacturer said in an intense voice. "Ten thousand women could use it with perfect safety——"

"And the ten thousand and first be stricken——"

"I found out about it myself only yesterday," Danisher said desperately. "Believe me, Mr. Norton, it's the solvent, just the solvent." His voice was hoarse. "I ordered every ounce of that solvent destroyed at once."

"It is a fact, though, that fifty thousand jars of cream went out of your factory in the ten days you used this particular solvent?"

Danisher's mouth jerked.

Norton nodded. "And *Fact* prints the facts, Danisher."

"It may have been a fact," Danisher broke in. "I'm not disputing that. But I've taken steps——"

"How long have you been manufacturing cosmetics?"

"We've used that solvent only ten days. It wasn't our fault. The samples——"

"The samples *we* analyzed were purchased in a Broadway store. They came from your factory day before yesterday. Is that not right, Mr. Henderson?"

Henderson nodded.

Danisher's eyes beneath their overhanging brows were opaque. "You know that to print that will ruin me? You know that only one woman in ten thousand runs any risk——?"

"I'm sorry, Danisher," Norton broke in evenly. He smiled. "No other publication in the world would have the courage to print the facts about one of its most profitable advertisers. *Fact* has that courage, Danisher. *Fact* is telling the women of America——"

Danisher said hoarsely, "Even if you knew that I've destroyed the solvent, that——"

There was a sharp rap at the door and it burst open at once spilling the anxious Production Manager into the room. "Sorry, Mr. Norton," he threw at the desk, "but, my God," to Henderson, "you can't put a double truck in place of that story. Cuts a third of a column too short."

"There is no time to change now," Norton was saying regretfully to Danisher. "Isn't that right, Baird?"

"The book's closing," Henderson agreed without looking up from the dummy over which his pencil was hovering.

The Production Manager gave Danisher a scornful glance. "Christ himself couldn't unlock those forms."

Norton's ready frown flitted. He said, "So you see, Danisher, we——"

"I've recalled every one of those jars," Danisher rasped, his gaunt face flaming. Then, as Norton's impassive face did not change, the manufacturer suddenly whirled and left the room.

The Production Manager hurried out immediately after him, grimly studying the form Henderson had blue-penciled.

Before the door clicked softly shut behind him, a gong rang five times. The clamor beyond the corridor diminished perceptibly.

Henderson drew a deep breath, dropped on the arm of a scarlet leather chair, and felt wearily for his pipe.

He said, "Well, another issue washed up." When Norton did not speak, Henderson looked at him. "Started something, haven't we, Phil?"

"You mean Danisher?"

"That was the name," Henderson agreed. He felt for his tobacco pouch, failed to find it, and got up from the chair arm.

"I presume we can handle Danisher," Norton said easily. Then, "You're through, Baird?"

Henderson rubbed his cheek and yawned suddenly. "Hope so."

"How about a drink?"

Henderson shook his head. "Sorry. Date." He looked ironically at Norton. "I hope you know what you've started, Phil."

"I think I do."

"Fine."

Henderson went out, still searching pockets for

the missing pouch.

Norton rose and stared out over the city, sweltering under its heat haze.

Clark Malory, coming into the office, said, "Mr. Norton."

Norton turned. "What, Clark?"

"Will there be anything else?"

Norton smiled suddenly. "Mr. Flint told you, I believe, Clark, that there would be no time clock."

"Yes."

"The editorial staff of *Fact* is expected to quit at five o'clock one day a week, Clark. One day only, Wednesday."

"I know, Mr. Norton." Malory was not amused at the traditional jest. "On Wednesdays they may quit at five because on Wednesdays they do not work. I know, Mr. Norton."

"Why do you want to go, Clark?"

The boy hesitated an instant. Then an irrepressible eagerness showed through his man-of-the-world manner. "Mr. Flint and Mr. Henderson are going to meet Monica Leeds for cocktails. Mr. Flint said I might go with him."

Norton smiled. "So you want to meet Monica Leeds? Why?"

"She is the greatest woman journalist in the country," scornfully.

Norton laughed. "You share Flint's opinion, I see."

"What if I do?"

"Don't be ashamed of it. It's a good opinion to share. Run along. I've some dictation I'd like you to do, some memos I don't want the secretaries to handle. I'll put it on cylinders, and you can come back tonight and get it out." He waved his hand. "Run along and touch the hem of the Leeds skirt."

III

HEAT, harsh, implacable heat of sun on steel and mortar, hung sluggish in the street. Idled motors, clotting at intersections, charged the air with gasoline reek; flat oily fumes of asphalt blanketed the pavement; from sweltering shops there seeped a medley of odors, of heat-ripened fruit, spilled beer, the tough dry smell of leather, the limp sickishness of drugs.

Monica Leeds, sitting by a curtained window that walled out the heat and made the Chatham Bar an oasis of cool washed air, stared into the broiling street outside. A certain angular stubbornness in her face grew more pronounced, highlighted by the interest that burned now in her gray eyes. They were eyes whose animation was quick, spontaneous, matching fluently the play of humor about her mouth, intelligent, shrewd, their lambent liveliness a foil to the stubborn line of jaw and chin. Although her daily column was syndicated to twenty-two of the country's leading newspapers, Monica Leeds conformed neither in mien nor manner with the conventional sketch of the woman journalist. Wholly individual, she required neither artifice nor affectation to signalize this. She was thirty-three, unmarried, and, by reason of a career which had been wholly satisfying, unresentful of either fact.

She looked up as three men came toward her table, Baird Henderson tall, loose, his hands riding the pockets of a tweed jacket, his tired eyes deep in their bony hollows warm and bright as they rested on her, Hugh Flint beside him looking sharply over the room, nodding as the occupants of a dozen tables here and there greeted him with gestures. Behind them walked Clark Malory, his youthful mouth scornful, his eyes adolescent lamps of deference.

Monica Leeds held out her hand. "Hello, Baird." She added, her voice neutral, "How do you do, Mr. Flint."

Hugh Flint's nervous features eased in a quick smile, his restless eyes lighting, his thin lips compressing immediately as an expression of pain leaped afresh into his uneasy eyes. Henderson, watching, saw Clark Malory wince with sympathetic anguish as he caught the unguarded twinge in Flint's face.

"Mind awfully our butting in like this?" Flint asked, his voice staccato.

"Not at all."

"This is Mr. Malory, Miss Leeds."

Monica smiled on The Future Editor of *Fact,* said pleasantly, "I've read about Mr. Malory."

Clark Malory swallowed and his mouth forgot for

a moment to be scornful. "That's awfully kind of you."

"Not at all," Monica said in a tone that dismissed him. She turned to Henderson. "Finished?"

"Don't we look it?"

"You're sure Clark and I aren't intruding?" Flint protested. "Perhaps the two of you——"

"Please. I'm flattered." She smiled. "There is a popular myth that Baird and I enjoy being alone. It has absolutely no basis in fact, has it, Baird?"

Henderson grunted, rubbed his eyes.

Flint said, "I didn't know."

The unsureness that marked his words reflected from his manner in its nervous, brittle urgency. Clark Malory, watching him closely, tore his glance away and gazed around the room with a worldly eye. Henderson chuckled to himself, knowing what the youth was thinking. At the Stork Club there might have been classmates to stare enviously, push over for introductions. It was too bad. The youth's eyes kept returning to Monica, who ignored him.

As if in response to Flint's tension, Monica's own bearing underwent a barely perceptible change. The neutrality of her tone when she had spoken to him was communicated to her eyes, to the firm line of her mouth.

Of the four, only Henderson seemed unaffected. He stretched his long legs under the table, rubbed his angular cheekbone. He asked, "Waiting long, Monica?" without concern.

"Rather." There was an unaccustomed edge to her voice. The next instant, on the point of softening the complaint, she threw a quick look at Henderson, and then returned her attention to Flint as if drawn by some insistent polar antagonism.

A waiter came, ornamental in gold braid, and took their orders. The unstable silence descended again. Henderson knew Monica was annoyed that he had brought Flint to the rendezvous. Henderson himself was annoyed, but not to the point of active resentment at Flint; and, because he knew both of them so well, his annoyance became merely the indifferent warp on which was woven the pattern of his speculation concerning the mission that had brought Flint with him, a mission whose successful issue was, Henderson decided, studying Monica Leeds' gray neutral eyes and stubborn jaw, a very doubtful thing. This gave him a wry, secret pleasure.

"Your column on the Anglo-American question, Miss Leeds," Flint said suddenly, "was fine, fine. I've been wanting to tell you."

"Thank you," coolly.

"You've a great gift," Flint continued nervously. "You see things clearly. You present them objectively. Women readers of your column must have a new pride in their sex. You interpret events so sanely, without the bias that—" He broke off.

"Without the bias you'd expect a woman to have?" The edge in Monica's tone had sharpened.

Flint made a nervous gesture. "When I say that you seem to think like a man, that you write like a man, you understand I'm paying you a compliment, don't you?"

"Yes, I believe I do."

"I say," Flint broke in, turning from her to Henderson, "since I've interrupted this tête-à-tête, why don't you two let me atone? How about coming out to my place on the Island for dinner tonight? We'll have a swim as soon as we get there."

Monica looked at Henderson. "That would be nice, wouldn't it, Baird?"

"Yes?" The question was metallic.

Henderson raised his eyebrows. He said good-humoredly, "It sounds like an idea."

"Then you'll come," Flint rushed on. "Splendid. Fly out, you know. Ship's down at the Wall Street float. Shall we say six? There?" He turned to Clark Malory. "Too bad you have to go back to the office, Clark. Some other time."

Anguish showed for an instant in the collegian's unguarded expression. Flint said eagerly to Monica, "Shall we say six, then?"

Monica said, "No," with sudden emphasis. "I've just remembered," she explained, "that Lynch Rains' is going to give a radio talk at six o'clock. I want to hear him."

Flint's narrow face flexed. "Why?"

"Curiosity."

"We can start earlier then," Flint conceded with a stiffness that barely failed to be ungracious.

"There is a radio in the cabin. Five-forty-five? Good. I'll meet you there."

Clark Malory gulped the cherry from his Manhattan and rose with Flint. He said, "It's been splendid, meeting you, Miss Leeds."

Monica smiled.

When the others had gone, Henderson asked,

"Why be brutal to the infant?"

"I don't like spoiled undergraduates."

"He's pretty foul. He may improve."

"If he gives me a chance at his education," Monica promised, "he will."

"He thinks you're God's personal contribution to American journalism."

Monica's brows arched. "He is much more modest than he appears."

Henderson chuckled. "You were probably an afterthought on God's part. As nearly as the young cub can, he worships the ink in Flint's pen."

"I sensed that."

"Hugh says the youngster's 'fact-minded' and one in a million. Malory follows Flint around with his mouth open. The rest of us," he chuckled again, "are simply Flint's pawns, even Phil. That doesn't sit too well with Phil, who reminds Clark now and then that he's president of Fact, Incorporated. Phil tolerates Clark, the way he tolerates all Hugh's enthusiasms." He paused. "Sorry about tonight. Maybe the swim will be worth it."

"What a curious way to issue an invitation."

"Hugh's way."

"Did he come here with you just to ask the two of us to dinner?"

"After a fashion. He wants to talk to you." Henderson twisted the stem of his glass and went on, his words bantering, "That was a concession, my dear Monica. He hates to talk to women."

"You forget he just invited me to dinner."

"But only as the puissant female scribe."

"Why is he so anxious to talk to me?"

"Why do you want to listen to Lynch Rains to-night?"

"I don't know. Some of the things he's done, I don't like. But whether you like them or not, you've got to admit that he's done something for the workers. His unions have power, power that, in his hands, is tremendous."

"He came to see us this morning."

"Why?"

"Hugh had been talking about a series of labor pieces. Was going to have Rains do them."

"Was?"

"That seems to be the right tense."

"Then Flint has changed his mind?"

Henderson shrugged. "My guess is that Phil Norton did the mind-change."

"Why did Flint want the labor articles?"

"Hugh still likes to play at being the liberal."

"Well?"

"Liberalism means either an absence or a complete equilibrium of pressures. I'm a liberal." His eyes wrinkled. "Did you ever hear of a starving liberal?"

"Flint isn't starving."

"Or a *powerful* liberal?" He signaled a waiter, ordered another Martini for each of them.

"Go on."

"Another thing you haven't seen are the latest circulation figures on *Fact*. Because they won't be released for ten days. Well, when you do see those figures, you'll see that *Fact* sells five million copies every week."

She said, "Five million? Half again the circulation of the *Post*, seven times as much as *Time*. My God! You're not serious, Baird."

"I only know what I read in the balance sheets."

"Five million!"

"You asked me what Hugh Flint wanted Rains' labor articles for, and I said it was because Hugh still likes to pretend he's a liberal. But—this is my guess—the minute Phil Norton sanded the rails, Hugh stopped and back-tracked." He waved his hand, and all but upset the Martinis which their waiter was on the point of putting down.

He watched Monica's thoughtful eyes stray to the baking pavement where the slow crowds flowed.

"Hugh Flint and Phil Norton," Henderson went on, "are on their way to becoming molders of destiny. Hugh knows it. Norton doesn't give a damn for destiny. He wants a hundred million dollars. Hugh's different. Well, molders of destiny can talk like liberals but they can't, by God, *be* liberals. I take it Norton convinced Hugh of that. Anyway it was Norton who queered the deal with Rains this morning. Rains was sore as hell."

She stared at him, one level eyebrow cocked. "And what is *your* place in the—destiny-factory?"

Henderson grinned. "Good old Charlie, dependable old Charlie. Same, I suppose, as it was in college where Hugh and Phil mapped the campaigns and I buttonholed the captains and ran the mimeograph." He paused and looked at her with something at once contrite and challenging and defensive in his eyes. "I lack ambition, or haven't you told me that before?"

IV

FLINT was pacing the float beside his silver-winged amphibian when Monica Leeds and Henderson arrived tardily. Annoyance was sharp in his eyes, annoyance and something yet sharper which Henderson, knowing him, recognized.

"Migraine still bad, Hugh?" Henderson asked softly as he stood for an instant beside the other man after Monica had entered the cabin.

"Yes," the word as sharp, as passionless as an icicle.

Henderson dropped a hand on Flint's shoulder. "We can still call it off. Some other time?"

"No, damn it." The heel of Flint's hand smote his temple, and for an instant the pain leaped furiously past his defenses into his eyes.

Monica had not spoken beyond a greeting. Her gray eyes watched Flint intently as he took his seat at the controls and put out a quick, nervous hand. The staccato gesture smoothed abruptly as his narrow fingers touched the throttle, and it was as if contact with the machine gave him a sudden extrinsic stability, as if in that moment he became part of the beautifully articulated mechanism, responsive to it as the horseman to his mount.

Henderson, watching no less intently than Monica, saw the flush rise in Flint's narrow cheeks as the motor's idled coughing swelled to a roar, caught the flash of imperative pride behind the gesture with which Flint motioned to the attendant to close the door.

Flint raised one hand and closed down the throttle with the other. As the sound of the motor dwindled away, the plane was rolled gently down the float and into the water. Again the motor leaped into thunderous life. The ship trembled, poised for a bare instant between the lateral thrust of tide rip and the strong, exultant tug of the propeller, and then moved out across the dark, slow-swirling river. A spray of spume dashed up across the cabin windows; the plane, bumping lightly now, its keeled cutwater shearing gull-like wings of white froth from the uneven surface, sped forward.

The bumping ceased. The lead-colored water fell swiftly away, tilted as Flint banked, and then they were climbing a steep, invisible ramp, below which the towered buildings that rushed past on their left dropped ever lower. The sun was still high in the west and heat shimmered over the clustered piles, the swiftly flashing canyons of the cross streets, but in the plane's cabin it was already perceptibly cooler, the streams of air hissing in at the cowled vents actually cold.

Flint looked aside at Monica, and Henderson noticed how the strain had left his eyes, giving place to an expression almost tranquil.

"Like it?"

"I love it."

This matched enthusiasm gave Henderson a swift, troubled feeling, which he repressed by looking away, down at the city lying beneath them. Its outlines, sharp as any map, thrust like the prow of a ship into the Bay and disappeared northward into the blue, ambiguous heat haze. Remembering suddenly, he looked at the clock on the instrument panel. It was two minutes before six. Flint and Monica were talking of flying, given over wholly to an electric stimulus with which the very thrumming of the air was instinct.

Henderson watched the minute hand of the clock creep slowly over the meridian, move on. Hell Gate Bridge slipped below them, and the blue waters of the Sound widened, inviting, limitless.

Watching them both, for he sat a little toward the rear, Henderson considered the mission which had been in Flint's mind when he had proposed the outing, the flattery of Monica Leeds implicit in it. So sure, however, was he of Monica's inflexible independence, of the consistency of her decisions, that the thought of what might happen to the long-standing, vaguely defined relation between them should she accept Flint's coming offer, did not intrude itself now.

Yet—he looked again at the clock. The hand had moved through the whole quadrant. Monica had not noticed. Doubt rasped minutely within Henderson.

Not until Flint was banking into a long glide that would bring them down in the landlocked stillness of Oyster Bay did Monica suddenly break off and cry, "Oh," in consternation. "The talk," she said. "Lynch Rains. I wanted to listen."

"Time isn't up," Henderson told her, and as he caught her eyes for an instant and saw the defensive light that flashed into them, he knew a desire to chuckle. He was aware also of the way the plane faltered as Flint's hand jerked, of the adolescent flicker of disappointment that showed on his taut lips.

Flint turned a dial and in a moment, above the drone of the motor and the high thin wail of their sloped descent, a man's voice filled the cabin, resonant, deliberate.

"What I am telling you is not empty suspicion," the voice was saying. "Labor has never had, and does not yet have in this country, freedom to express its views. The organs of publication in America, whose editors boast of freedom, are without exception closed to labor. Religion, commerce, government, Wall Street—all have free access to the public prints, but the voice of labor is. . ."

The plane, dropping, grooved suddenly into the blue water and settled. A moment later they ran up on a shelving float, and a mechanic thrust chocks under the wheels.

Flint nodded absently to the mechanic, and, as all motion ceased, save for the paced revolving of the propeller, his hands grew restive on the controls. But, listening to the strong, unfaltering voice, he did not move. Henderson, watching Monica, saw that she was oblivious to all except the words that filled the cabin."

". . . the magazine I refer to is *Fact*. The editors of *Fact* advertise their freedom loudly, disclaim all bias, shout to their millions of readers that they are utterly without prejudice. Yet not twelve hours ago the editors of *Fact* revoked an agreement with organized labor for a series of articles presenting labor's attitude toward government-owned utilities. This action, on the part of one of the greatest national magazines, is thoroughly in keeping with precedent which goes back to the very founding of American journalism.

"It cannot longer be tolerated. Labor will no longer tolerate it. The time has come for an intelligent public opinion to confront the princes of privilege with their folly, demand they end their bitterly held monopoly on the instruments by which public opinion is expressed. The time has come for a sane, judicial settlement of this old grievance. It is for the American people to settle it."

The voice ended, its resonance dying reluctantly. Monica, her chin on her fist, stared sightlessly out over the cool, blue Bay. Flint leaned forward and turned a switch nervously as a nasal announcer broke in. Red burned in his narrow cheeks. He drew a quick breath. "Shall we have a dip before dinner?"

V

ENDERSON, long legs straight out before him, slouched in a basket chair and eyed the woman who sat between him and Flint. A full moon whitened the terrace where they sat, made the night a luminous amphitheater for the song of cricket and cicada, the light swift play of the summer wind. In the distance, where the shore curved, the lights of Oyster Bay twinkled.

Abruptly, Hugh Flint spoke. *"Fact* is edited by men, Miss Leeds," he said rapidly. "That has been its strength. But we've come to the point where we need something else."

"A woman's magazine," Monica said.

Flint moved forward in his chair. "Exactly. And we're ready for it. I've had two research groups canvassing women in seven states. I know what three million women read, what they serve for breakfast, what churches they attend, what they think of prize fighting, communism, the cost of shoes, crop control, the yellow peril, contraceptives. Women control seventy per cent of this country's wealth. Directly or indirectly, they spend fifty-eight per cent of the national income, cast potentially forty-nine and a fraction per cent of the national ballot. There is a vast fallow field we haven't touched."

"Women read *Fact* now."

"Inadequately, Miss Leeds. I'm being frank. *Fact* is written and edited from a masculine viewpoint. Women read it, yes, but without getting the direct forceful stimulus they should. Why? Because their point of view is slighted. I want a magazine built on a foundation of feminine logic, geared to the *thoughts* of women. Only a woman can do that. You can do it, Miss Leeds. You've an understanding of women, and a masculine clarity and directness." Flint stopped. Then he broke out, "With us, you can be the most powerful woman in America!"

"Perhaps I am not interested in being the most powerful woman in America."

"Nonsense."

"Power in the abstract does not appeal to me."

"A power for good, then."

"Still an abstraction."

"A power for education," intensely.

"Better. But what kind of education?"

"Education in living. Sharpening of perception firing a keen appetite for the truth, provoking thought, giving to women the same perspective on world events that *Fact* is giving to men, millions of men."

"Women, intelligent women, use the same logic as men, Mr. Flint."

(There could be no doubt, Henderson thought. Within her some inner spring of excitement had

been broached, some keenly sensitive response elicited. There was a mounting warmth in her voice, in
the way she turned in her chair to face Flint, leaning toward him across its arm.)

"Intelligent women, yes." Flint pounced on the
word. "But what about the great majority, the unin-
telligent? Think what you can do with them, knowing their superstitions, their limitations, their bias,
molding them——"

"Propagandizing them?"

"Not at all, not at all," nettled. "Giving them the
truth."

"But the truth colored to make it palatable to
them?"

In the moonlight slanting over the terrace Henderson saw Flint flush. "The truth cannot be colored, Miss Leeds. It is what it is."

There was a short, strained silence. Flint broke
it. His voice was lower. His passion had changed
key, become minor, persuasive.

"Let me tell you about *Fact*, Miss Leeds, about
how *Fact* came into being. When Phil Norton and I
were graduated from Harvard. . ."

(Henderson, sinking into his moody reverie, reflected: "Yes, when the *three* of us were graduated
from Harvard, you and Phil were campus big men,
weren't you? You had managed class politics for
eight years, first at Groton and then at Harvard, between you steered caucus, debate, and committee
smoothly into channels you chose, between you
been a government whose sanction was noblesse
oblige? And when we left Harvard there was a conference, unlike the conferences that had deter-

mined undergraduate policy only in that the future
of a nation and not a club was at stake. The nation
was unaware of this, but you weren't, were you?"
Remembering, Henderson thought how Flint and
Norton had gravely discussed politics—and rejected
the field as beneath them; they had considered industry—adjudged it unexciting and pedestrian; fi-
nance had beckoned, but was renounced—after six
months' apprenticeship in the firm of Norton père--
as lacking in scope that they were seeking.)

"Phil was in Europe," Flint was saying. He had
risen and was sitting on the low stone balustrade,
his dropped shoulders throwing his weight hard on
the heels of his hands, his head bent toward
Monica, his manner magnetic, earnest. "I was reading Thomas Jefferson that summer. One night—it
was the seventh of June, 1923—I found words
which exploded in my mind like a bomb. 'The people are the only safe repositories of power. And to
render them even safer, their minds must be improved.' " He paused a moment, repeated slowly,
"Their minds must be improved." Another pause. "I
remembered another: 'The engine is the press.' I
knew at once what we wanted. I cabled Phil twenty
minutes later, and sat down that night to draw up
the plan of *Fact*. I worked through until the next
noon. Even one of my headaches, which up until
that night would have tangled my thoughts into a
lunacy of pain, failed to stop me. Nothing could
stop me. Feverishly, blindly, I crushed that headache, and knew that something more powerful than
the pain was in what I was doing.

"The newspapers, I told myself, where they present all the news—as in the *Times*—they sacrifice personalities and human interest. Where they exploit human interest—as in the tabloids and local dailies in the provinces—they present the news so sketchily that no reader can know the facts. *Fact*, I told myself, will present the *whole* of the news in its context of living humanity. It will not distort, conceal, truckle. Its pages will be—not reflect vaguely— the history of today. From that ideal I have never swerved—Fact, Incorporated has never swerved."

He told how *Fact* took its place the following March on the newsstands, thin for want of advertising, but with the leanness of a prophet burning-eyed from the desert. How at first it was amateurish, unsure of its destiny. How for three disheartening years he and Norton—Norton the practical businessman with the pragmatist's doubt of all idealism, lover of organization and efficiency, *Fact's* sapient figurehead and restraining balance wheel— how he and Norton had struggled against appalling odds. How in September of the fourth year something had hapened: the circulation curve flexed upward overnight into an hyperbola, the thin, sacerdotal tone of the prophet swelled into a triumphant shout, two million readers ready at last to be given the truth.

"Since then," Flint concluded, and after his long, impassioned monologue his voice was weary, "we have gone steadily ahead. We have gone ahead as far as we can go in one direction. We must blaze a new trail. I want *you* to blaze that trail, Miss Leeds. We can put behind you all the power, the prestige and resources of Fact, Incorporated."

But the fire had gone from his words. The repetition of his urgency was ashen, without the dominant assurance that had marked his opening. When Monica did not reply at once, Flint slipped off the low wall and returned to drop into his chair, his hand pressed to his head.

"I'm sorry," Monica said gently. "I'm simply not interested, Mr. Flint. My work is exactly what I want now."

"I'd treble, quadruple your income." The offer was petulant.

Monica shook her head. "It's sufficient now, thank you."

(Henderson thought, "It is twice mine now.")

The silence lasted longer this time. The light wind rippled through ivy blanketing the wall behind them. A bobwhite called.

Flint leaned forward to pour a drink with trembling hand, found the decanter empty, and rose. He said, "Excuse me." Frustration and the pain racking his head made the words stiff and artificial.

"Is he always such a poor loser?" Monica asked at length after Flint had gone into the house.

"He hasn't lost—yet."

"I'm not going to change my mind."

"Perhaps you don't know."

"Look here, Baird," she said intensely, turning to him. "I've told you why I won't work for Hugh Flint and Phil Norton."

"Why don't you tell him?"

"He wouldn't understand."

"No," Henderson agreed, "he wouldn't understand."

After a pause, Monica said slowly, "Think what could be done, though, with five million readers. Think what a power for stability and honesty——"

"Um." Henderson's tone was ironical.

"If you had a free hand," quickly.

"Who has?"

"No one, of course. But there are degrees of bondage." She added intensely: "There's something wretchedly dishonest about pretending to have no bias on any subject. Truth—at least truth about human problems and human conflicts—isn't worked out on an adding machine."

Flint returned with the decanter, poured three drinks in silence. Then he began talking rapidly about a Percheron stallion he had purchased the day before, outlining his system of breeding, discoursing brilliantly on the history of the strain. It was as if he barraged them with words to cover his retreat.

Henderson was acutely aware of the other's condition, recognized the symptoms of the gnawing pain behind Flint's fever-struck eyes. Moved suddenly by a sympathy he could not account for, he was on the point of suggesting that he and Monica return to the city, when he caught sight of the lights of a car racing along the country road bordering the meadow.

It disappeared behind a clump of trees, but in a moment its lights swept across the lawn, and those on the terrace heard gravel churn as it slid to a stop in front of the house.

VI

SHORTLY before twelve that August night, Julia Norton put down her book, yawned, stretched back against the cushions of the chartreuse chaise longue, and arched her white wrist, frowning at her watch. Ten years younger than her husband, there was the willfulness of ripe youth in her red mouth. Her eyes, beneath the deftly penciled slant of brow were crystalline. When she swung her feet to the floor, there was the same hint of something crystalline, imperative in the taut slenderness of her body as she arched her back and stretched again. Frowning, she fished with bare foot for a mule fallen under the seat, walked to her dressing table, and took the telephone from beneath the ruffled skirt of a Versailles milkmaid.

She called a number in the city and waited. Into the phone she said, "Is Mr. Flint still in the office? . . . Thank you." After a moment her scarlet mouth grew sullen. "Oh, he has? . . . Is Mr. Norton there, then? . . . What? . . . No, no message, thank you."

She pressed the switch in the phone's cradle and

36

called another number, waited, said, "Is Mr. Flint there?" After a moment's wait, "Hugh, what are you doing at home? I thought you and Phil planned to stay in town. . . . Oh, you have? Who?" Listening, her eyes changed slowly, tiny brackets etching at the corners of her mouth. "Oh no, Hugh, it's late. . . . No, it's too late, and anyway you have guests. . . . No, see you tomorrow morning. Tennis maybe. . . . Um. . . . Night."

She replaced the telephone and sat for a moment staring into her mirror. Then she rose, stripped off the dressing gown and regarded her naked body in a triple mirror. For a moment she stood with knotted breath and then exhaled suddenly. She went about dressing with a deliberate, unflurried haste.

When she had dressed, she took a light tweed coat from its closet and with the coat over her arm went downstairs, out of the house. Moonlight whitened the lawn, glistened on the swept stones of the driveway, made cool caverns of darkness under elms in which the night wind whispered. At the garage, she threw back the door and entered the oil-scented quiet. She stepped into her coupe and switched the lights on dim. With her hand on the key she heard the garage door swing gently in an eddy of the wind, and, murmuring to herself angrily, got out of the car to walk back and drop the bolt that would hold it open.

Then, with her hand on the door of the car, ready to step in again, she halted. The whisper of the wind-ruffled elms intensified the quiet. The sound which had checked her came again, a furtive, intimate noise near at hand, the shuffle of a shoe on gravel.

She reached into the car and flicked the lights bright. As the glowing circles flashed up, the room bloomed into radiance. Julia stepped back, stiffened, and called sharply, "Who's there?"

In the wide doorway stood a man, tall, gaunt, his sunken cheeks gray, his colorless, unquiet eyes beneath their furze of brow fixing on her, moving unsurely to the car, returning.

Julia demanded, "What do you want?"

The man's bony hands twitched at a button on his coat. Julia saw they were empty. She took a step toward him and bent swiftly to seize a hammer leaning against the wall.

The man in the door retreated, turned and broke into a shuffling run down the driveway. Julia, following him into the moonlight, watched him disappear between the pillars at the road. She started toward the house, stopped, and went back to the car. A moment later she whirled the coupé about on the graveled apron before the garage and sped down the drive to skid narrowly between the pillars into the highroad.

A hundred yards away she turned down a rutted country lane, emerged after a space on pavement once more, and swung the little car hard to the left under a wrought-iron gate to speed up a curving drive and slide to a stop before Hugh Flint's Georgian house.

She jumped out of the car, ran up to the door which stood open to the sweetness of the country night, and across the austerity of hall and foyer to the drawing room. At the entrance she checked herself. The room was in shadow save for a cone of yellow light where a lamp shed radiance over an empty chair at the far end near open doors leading to the moonlighted terrace.

VII

A CHAIR scraped when she stood in the doorway. Hugh Flint's sharp voice rose nervously from the silence.

"Julia, hello. Come join us. Mrs. Norton, may I present Monica Leeds. Nice of you to drop in, Julia. Tom Collins? Scotch?"

Henderson rose to his lank height and asked (finding a grim satisfaction in the innuendo), "Late for a call, what, Julia?"

"Oh, hello Baird. Irish if you have it, Hugh. How do you do, Miss Leeds. I'm so glad to . . . Don't let me interrupt, *please*." She sank into a chair. "I need a drink the worst way. I just finished running a tramp off our place," she added lightly. "Don't mind me if I'm a little flighty."

Pressed by the others she said, laughing, "Oh, nothing happened, nothing at all. There was simply this creature standing in the garage door leering at me when I got out of the car. 1 picked up a hammer and he ran. That's all really. Don't stand there staring at me, Hugh darling. I'm parched."

"You went after him with a hammer?" Monica

asked.

"I'd have preferred a jack handle," Julia confessed. "It was awfully short, that hammer."

When Flint had gone for the whiskey, Julia turned impulsively toward the woman sitting between her and Henderson. "I've heard so much about you, Miss Leeds. I'm sure Phil thinks you're the shrewdest woman in New York. Frankly I've been afraid he and Hugh would break down and decide to have a woman editor. I'd be consumed with jealousy, I know."

Before Monica could parry this astonishing tribute, Julia hurried on, "Oh dear, did I say I wanted Irish whiskey? How silly. I'll catch Hugh and head him off. He'll be furious."

Her heels clicked on the flagstones and she disappeared into the drawing room.

Monica Leeds murmured, "My God."

"She's at a disadvantage—finding you here like this."

"Finding me here? Here?"

"Must I diagram it?" Henderson asked.

"Oh."

"She's usually more discreet. You threw her off stride. My being here didn't help. She hates me only slightly less than she hates Phil Norton."

"Why doesn't Norton divorce her?"

"Because of the scandal, probably. I don't know. He's a Calvinist on the subject of scandal."

"Then why doesn't *she* divorce him?"

"Because she knows Phil would spend every cent he has to keep from paying her alimony." In a moment he added, "And she isn't sure Hugh Flint would marry her."

"How stupid." Then, "But why should she hate you?"

"I know all about it. I'm probably the only one who does. Being shameless, I'm telling you."

"I'm not exactly afire with gratitude."

"If you're going to be part of the family, you should know the skeletons."

"But I'm not."

"Perhaps."

A maid appeared at the door. "Mr. Flint, please."

"He's inside," Henderson told her. "He may be some time. We can give him a message."

"Oh, thank you, sir. But Mr. Norton is calling from the city."

Henderson jackknifed his long legs and rose. He said, "I'll talk to him."

When he returned he stood in the doorway a moment before stepping down to the flagstones. Monica turned her head and looked at him, her brows rising.

"Both my distinguished superiors," Henderson said, his voice tinged with disgust, "have the whimseys tonight. Phil phones he's bringing Lynch Rains out to spend the night at his house."

"Bringing Lynch Rains out——?"

"I told you," Henderson went on, perching on the low stone wall before her, "that Lynch Rains came into the office this morning. Hugh had been dickering with him to do some pieces giving organized labor's slant on the TVA. I told you that deal fell through."

"Norton objected?"

"Quite possibly. Anyway it was Norton who told Rains the deal was off. I happened to be with Phil when Rains came in. I'm not sure Hugh even knew he was there."

"Could Norton have ordered Flint to drop the plan for the articles?"

Henderson shook his head. "Not ordered. Hugh has just as much actual power in *Fact* as Norton. But Hugh might have given in as a concession of some kind. Anyway, Phil told Rains that *Fact* didn't want anything of his, and Rains pointed out the feeling was mutual. He mentioned in particular the way *Fact* has been handling the Mifflin strike."

"*Fact*," Monica observed, "has been handling the Mifflin strike with its usual unbiased, detached, objective candor."

"Phil mentioned that to Rains—suavely."

"But no man likes to be called a murderer," Monica added. "Even a 'Napoleonic murderer.' Even Lynch Rains probably doesn't like to be called a murderer."

"You get it. Phil pointed out that the strikers *had* committed murder, and when Rains asked what in God's name the company guards and strikebreakers had done, Phil said that much as he deplored justifiable homicide and the use of force as an instrument of economic justice——"

"No!"

"Phil's words. Rains said, 'Murder is a crime, Mr. Norton,' and Phil smiled like a grammarian and said, 'Exactly, Rains. I'm glad you see our point. Murder is a fact, to be presented as such. *Fact* presents facts.' "

Monica said thoughtfully, "I think I like your Mr. Norton even less than I like your Mr. Flint."

"Wait a minute," Henderson said, and put his hand into his pocket. "Listen to this. This," he shook a paper at her, "was to have been *Fact's* cold, uncolored aseptic account of current events in one corner of the globe this week."

He unfolded the page, held it in the moonlight and read: "Guerrilla war flared again on Monday in Mifflin. For fourth consecutive week steelworkers leaving World Steel's plant in Mifflin were ambushed by strikers, attacked, two murdered, several wounded. Plant officials repeated their refusal to confer with union boss Lynch Rains until he disarms his marauders. . . ."

"Marauders!" Monica choked.

Henderson folded the paper and put it away.

"*Fact* isn't printing that, is it Baird?"

"No," Henderson said. "It was too much for my bowels. 1 told Phil it was kill this or get a man to take my place."

Flint, carrying a tray with bottles, came out on the terrace.

Henderson said, "Phil just called to say he's on his way out with Rains."

The bottles clinked as Flint's hand jerked. "Bringing Rains out here?" Flint demanded, incredulous.

"That's what he said."

Julia hurried through the door, said, "Hugh, *please* don't be such a fool. You've simply got to——"

"What else did he say?" Flint asked, his voice tight.

"He wants to get together with you and Rains and talk things out. My guess is he heard what Rains said——"

"Splendid," Flint burst out. "Splendid! I knew Phil would come around if—" He broke off, turned to Monica. "You'll want to be there, Miss Leeds when——"

"Hugh," Julia wailed. She took his arm. "You simply mustn't do things like this, Hugh. You've got to go to bed." She made an imploring gesture to Monica and Henderson. "Hugh really needs a nurse at times like this. He's got a temperature of a hundred and one, and I know that migraine will kill him sometime."

"Julia!" Flint interrupted. His hand strayed unconsciously to his forehead as he grimaced in a wave of pain. "I'll tell you what I'll do."

"What?" doubtfully.

"I'll go up and lie down for half an hour. Want to be as clear as possible." His voice was unsteady. "Make yourselves comfortable, won't you? Sorry." He turned abruptly and left them, Julia trailing behind him.

"That," Henderson said when they were gone, "was probably one of the worst shocks Hugh ever got. I don't wonder he wants a breathing space. It may represent something of a triumph for him if he can persuade Phil to—" He did not finish the sentence. A moment later he looked up as a light went on in a window just above. They could hear Julia's solicitous murmur.

"Baird, I must get back to town. I don't feel up to any more crises tonight." Monica rose.

The light in the room above went off. As they stepped into the drawing room from the terrace, Julia hurried toward them.

"Not going? Oh, please don't go."

"I'm sorry, Mrs. Norton."

"Hugh seemed to think you'd want to see this Rains person."

"Perhaps he can arrange it for us in town sometime. I must return to the city."

"Oh, I feel foul about spoiling things here," Julia said. "It's just that it's insane for Hugh to go on as he——"

"I'm sure it's very sensible of you," Monica said evenly. Then to Henderson, "Ready?"

VIII

AT Julia's direction, Grey, Flint's chauffeur, brought a roadster from the garage. The last train had left an hour before.

As they rode away from the severely ostentatious house, Monica said, "Now I've had my view of the promised land."

"You'll learn to like it."

"I'm even less interested than I might have been."

"Why?"

"For one thing, I shouldn't like a complication like that behind my back."

"Like what?"

"Julia."

"She's harmless."

"She is not harmless. She's an irresponsible little opportunist—like her husband and Hugh Flint. If you want to know why I wouldn't work for *Fact*, Baird, there's the reason in a capsule. I don't like opportunists." She shook her head and stared out over the moon-silvered countryside. "How can *you* stomach it?"

"Habit," Henderson said.

"Seriously, though, Baird?"

He was silent a moment. Then he said slowly, "You can get used to anything. Your sense of values dulls, I suppose."

"That doesn't sound like you."

"And now and then," he went on, ignoring her, "I can do something that gives me back my self-respect."

"They've treated you shabbily," she burst out. "You're as good as either of them and they've kept all the rewards themselves and doled you out——"

"I didn't mean keeping my self-respect that way. I meant something that gives me the sense of being useful. I killed that story on the Mifflin trouble by myself. And yet, what good did *that* do?" he went on, his tone suddenly savage. "Kept all mention of the brutality out of our precious pages, dulled people's sense of the violence going on there. No news is good news. If you don't read about it in the papers, it didn't happen. All quiet on the Western Front. Hang the god-damned malcontents! Christ!"

She said quietly after a space, "That doesn't sound like you either. Why so bitter, Baird?"

"What else is there to be? The world heading for Armageddon."

"Is Armageddon a matter of days away?"

"It is."

"I refuse to be stampeded." She added, "Frankly I'm more concerned this minute with the triangle you showed me back there. If that woman decides to, she can have a more tragic effect on *Fact* and you, Baird Henderson, than Lynch Rains and all the——"

"How?"

"She's evil. She's unsatisfied and selfish, and she's got a kind of furious courage."

Henderson laughed.

"I'm serious," Monica protested.

After he had left Monica and put Flint's roadster away, Henderson walked for a while in the night-time streets, and as he walked, his depression deepened. The city was restless under the hot dome of the night, its breathing light and uneasy.

He thought of the desperation of the steelworkers sitting tense and sleepless behind barred doors in Mifflin, waiting perhaps for Lynch Rains to come from the city and hearten them, their desperation pierced by the wails of infants without milk. He thought of the stamping of the armed guard through the company streets, the brutal ring of hobnails on cobbles, the crash of shots, the fierce, white-hot hatred swelling higher and higher.

The buildings about him, dark, towering silently, grew ominous: they seemed to be waiting, waiting until the hour when the hatreds would flow together like rivulets of rain on a pane.

Imagining, Henderson saw the spit of smuggled rifles from the blind windows that rose on either side of the silent street, the jumbled barricades, heard the scream of sirens, shouts, the crashing volleys, saw jagged holes yawn in the blind, impassive walls, the slow collapse of all monuments.

And against the bitter panorama, like figures superimposed against some clever photomontage of carnage and destruction, he saw Norton and Flint striding, leading, urging on, coldly setting clique against clique, man against man, unleashing the torrents of hatred by their very passivity, goading to action by inaction, shrilling the conflict by their very obliquity—men of power, others like them, secure in the pious trappings of good will, the buckler of apparent rectitude and honor.

And because he could not see Norton and Flint against this background without sly, mordant glimpses of himself not far behind, he savagely turned his thoughts away and went home to troubled sleep under the breathless night, plagued by dreams in which Julia Norton, like a maenad, drove cringing men before her with an upraised hammer.

He awoke unrefreshed, with the sense of something portentous hanging by a thread—and walked to his window to look down on the newsstand below, where the headlines in the tabloids shrieked up at him.

Philip Norton, President of Fact, Incorporated, had been found murdered in a country lane a short distance from his home.

IX

THE NEWSPAPERS, motivated by that singularly pure *esprit de corps* which gives any tragedy within the fourth estate the status of a national catastrophe, made of Philip Norton's murder a *cause célèbre* in six hours.

From early morning, tense-voiced announcers interrupted radio programs to bring to a listening nation bulletins announcing the emergence of this or that slim clue, descriptions of the police planes scouring the low Nassau County skies, the white police cars dashing here and there about the countryside.

By early afternoon, as the hour for the inquest approached, roads in the vicinity of the murder lane were choked with the curious, and a steady stream of cars flowed slowly past the village mortuary where Norton's body lay.

Baird Henderson, driving Flint's roadster, was caught in the traffic which moved like a glacier along the village street. To Clark Malory, who sat beside him, he said, "We'll be lucky if we find a place to park."

The youth had been unusually silent during the hot drive from the city. His narrow face was pale, his disdainful mouth set. He asked, "You don't honestly think he is?"

Henderson, fuming at the traffic, said absently, "Is what?" He looked sharply at Clark. "You're still worrying about that?"

"I'm a realist," the youth snapped. He bit his lip. "It's common knowledge that Flint is ten times more important in *Fact* than Norton was."

"Flint's in no danger."

"They killed Norton."

Henderson's mouth tightened. He said quietly, "Someone killed him. It may have nothing to do with *Fact*."

"Don't be naïve, Henderson."

The phrase nettled Henderson, but he held his peace.

"*Fact* has enemies, Henderson," Clark went on condescendingly. "I've been in a position to know that. Two men were in the office yesterday who—" He broke off. "Flint should have a bodyguard."

"How good a shot are you?" Henderson asked.

Clark was oblivious to his irony. "I broke ninety in meets in high school. That was with a .22," he added. "I've never handled a police caliber."

Silence lasted until, after what was almost a physical assault on the sweating local constable, Henderson established their right to turn into an alley and stop half a block from the hall where the inquest would be held.

Clark spoke once more as they walked toward

the building. "Will we—that is, will the body be—"

Henderson said, "No."

Women in sunglasses and halter brassieres hung from the slowly passing cars and stared at them curiously as they entered the hall. It had been broiling in the street; the low barren room was an oven, shades drawn at the windows to keep out prying glances, naked electric bulbs hanging from green cords and shedding a stifling brightness on the officials, witnesses, and newsmen who crowded in.

Henderson's eyes widened as he recognized Julia Norton sitting beside Flint. She was veiled. Flint's narrow face was taut and ashen. Beyond Julia sat a slim dark-faced man in uniform whom Henderson recognized as Flint's chauffeur, Grey. At the other side of an open space, Henderson saw Lynch Rains between two lawyers. The labor leader's square, black-browed face was impassive.

The preliminary formalities were brief. The first witness examined was a veterinary, whose name Henderson did not hear. Punctilious, perspiring, the veterinary told how he had been on his way along the lane about three o'clock that morning and discovered Norton's body. No, he had not lingered beyond that hasty examination, but had sped to the nearest police booth to give the alarm.

The two officers of the radio car who had responded were next questioned. The jack handle which had been used to crush Norton's skull was produced and identified by one of the officers. They were excused.

Flint was questioned. He told in a low tense

voice how he and his guests had sat conversing on the terrace, of the telephone call which Henderson had answered, of how he had retired with a headache and been awakened shortly before four by his chauffeur who told of Norton's death.

Henderson heard his own name. He stood up, told what Norton had said over the phone to him, verified what Flint had already recounted.

Lynch Rains' name was called. He rose, his square face unmoving, his deep voice steady. "Here."

"Mr. Rains, it is reported that you were riding out from the city with Mr. Norton."

"I was."

The room was suddenly breathless, parching heat forgotten. This forthright answer threw the dapper questioner out of his stride. He removed his glasses, wiped them, clamped them again on his short nose. Lynch Rains waited calmly.

"Well, Mr. Rains, will you tell us just exactly what happened?"

"I rode with Mr. Norton as far as——"

"Where did you meet him?"

"On the corner of Fifty-third Street and Lexington Avenue."

"By prearrangement?"

"Accidentally."

Again the hush was palpitant.

"What do you mean by that?"

"I was crossing Lexington. I heard my name called. Mr. Norton motioned to me. He was waiting for the traffic light to change. I stepped over to his car. We talked for a moment, and he asked me to ride out to the country with him."

"You talked for a moment?"

"Yes."

"What about?"

Rains looked at him steadily. "Of what importance is that?"

The questioner took a step toward Rains, removed his glasses, and gestured with them. "Could
it have been about the remarks you made in your
radio speech last night?"

"It could have been," Rains answered calmly.

"Ah." The glasses went back into place. "Now
you say that Mr. Norton requested you to accompany him to his home?"

"He did."

"Why?" It was an explosion.

The room stirred.

"To talk," Rains answered.

"And you—did talk?"

"As far as Kew Gardens, yes."

"Ah. And what happened in Kew Gardens?"

"I got out of his car and went back to the city by
subway."

A fourth time tension crackled among the spec-
tators. "Perhaps you and Mr. Norton quarreled before——?"

The lawyer at Rains' right leaped to his feet.
"This is an inquest, not a grand jury," he said
sharply.

After a moment's whispered consultation with
his colleagues about the table, the interrogator allowed Rains to sit down.

A slack-jawed change-maker from the Union

Turnpike station in Kew Gardens told of seeing Rains enter the subway turnstile at approximately one o'clock the morning before.

"Mrs. Norton." The inquisitorial voice was soft.

Julia raised her hand.

"I am very sorry, Mrs. Norton, but you understand how important it is that we——"

"I understand," in a low tone.

"Will you tell us all that you can, Mrs. Norton, please?"

"After Mr. Henderson and Miss Leeds left," Julia said steadily, "I sent for a nurse from New York. I was afraid Mr. Flint might be really ill. Then I asked Grey, his chauffeur, to wait with me until the nurse arrived. I was—uneasy, for some reason I could not explain. Grey and I talked about England as we sat on the terrace waiting. We spoke of people he had worked for in England, some of whom I knew. Once I went up and listened at Mr. Flint's door. He was sleeping. The police arrived just as I came downstairs."

"Thank you, Mrs. Norton. We appreciate your—-"

"There is something else," Julia said steadily.

The room quickened.

"Yes?"

"About midnight as I was going over to Mr. Flint's to meet Miss Leeds and Mr. Henderson, I encountered a prowler in our garage. I drove him out and he ran away."

"Could you describe this man, Mrs. Norton?"

Julia hesitated. "I think so."

"Will you, please?"

"He was tall. He wore a loose, gray coat and a

soft hat. He had a jutting chin and very bushy eyebrows. That is all I can remember."

Henderson heard Clark Malory gasp beside him.

"That is a great deal, Mrs. Norton. You were very observant in a crisis. Is there anything else?"

Julia shook her veiled head.

Two hours after the interrogation began, reporters rushed out of the building to call their papers and announce that Norton had been murdered by person or persons unknown.

Henderson and Clark Malory waited by the door for Flint and Julia. "Did you hear what she said?" the youth demanded.

Henderson nodded.

"The man was Danisher."

"You think so?"

"My God, I know it was! He threatened Norton yesterday evening in the office. I heard him. Flint *is* in danger."

Julia and Flint came through the doorway. Seeing Henderson, she took his arm. "Thanks, Baird," she said softly, "for being here."

Henderson wondered what prompted her ambiguous gratitude. His curiosity was brief, for at that instant Lynch Rains emerged. The chunky labor leader would have passed Flint without a sign had not Flint put out his hand.

Rains stopped, looked squarely at Flint.

Flint said steadily, "I am quite satisfied, Rains," as reporters crowded up and cameras clicked. Flint's outstretched hand was imperious.

Rains took it. He said, "Thanks," gruffly, and walked on.

Henderson watched Rains go. He thought, "How easy it would be to jockey that man into the shadow of the gallows," and an obscure prescience turned within him as he walked with Julia, Flint, and Clark to where Grey waited beside a curtained limousine, beyond which a gaping crowd stood.

"Are you going to tell them," Clark demanded in a low hoarse voice, "or do I have to?"

"Julia," Henderson asked, "where will you be for the next two hours?"

"At home, Baird."

"Will you let me talk to you if I come there?"

Henderson caught Flint's sharp glance.

Julia said, "Of course, Baird."

Clark's eyes were on Flint. "May I come with you and Mrs. Norton?" he asked intensely.

Flint nodded and stepped into the limousine after Julia. The boy followed. Henderson drove rapidly back to the city, went to the office, and hurried down a corridor to *Fact's* library and reference room. The attendant found what he wanted at once, and five minutes later he was on his way back to Long Island.

Julia, pale, red-eyed, but composed, recognized the photograph at once.

"But, Baird," she asked, "who is it?"

Clark Malory, his youthful eyes flaming, his scornful mouth unsteady, burst out, *"Danisher.* He'll be after you next, Mr. Flint. He's a madman. He——"

"Danisher, of course," Flint said sharply. "He was in yesterday afternoon. He'll be picked up immediately."

But Danisher was not picked up immediately. To the chagrin of a score of police agencies and a detective bureau which Flint engaged the next morning, Danisher was not picked up at all. Sometime between midnight and morning he had vanished.

X

CLARK MALORY elected to stay with Flint when the three of them left, and Henderson, to his relief, found himself without a passenger. He drove out of the Norton grounds, and was on the point of turning to the right when an errant impulse made him spin the wheel and cut sharply into the road in the opposite direction.

A short distance away a police car was drawn up at the entrance to the lane in which Norton had been found dead. Henderson stopped, then walked over to the police car in which a sergeant was sitting. He talked with the sergeant for a time, established his identity, and received permission to drive down the lane.

It was not difficult to find the spot. Distastefully he stopped a short distance away and got out. The August sun was a red ball low in the west, and in the coolness of the trees by a rail fence a cloud of gnats pulsated. The dust odor of clover drifted down from the meadow. A quail broke from cover, looked at Henderson, and scuttled across the lane to a thicket.

Henderson walked about where other searchers had milled. There was nothing but the dusty beaten grass. He had expected no more, and was not disappointed. But a seedling of futility made itself felt as he returned at last to his car.

He did not get into the car. His eyes were caught by the glint of metal in the grass across the lane. He went around the car, and when he came to the spot where the metal glinted he knelt. A narrow band of chromium, brightly polished, lay six inches from a stump on which a stub projected the length of a man's finger. One side of the stub was freshly scraped.

Henderson picked up the bright band. It was less than six inches long, pointed at one end, and had been folded longitudinally so that the two edges matched; opened out flat it would be slightly more than half an inch wide. Henderson glanced up. He was a dozen yards from the spot where Norton's car had stood on the opposite side of the lane.

He saw the police car turn into the lane, and rose, slipping the narrow strip of metal into a pocket of Flint's roadster as he got in and started the motor.

When he reached New York and turned from the bridge into Second Avenue, a truck driver, hurtling out of his lane into an opening, misjudged the angle and wedged with a crash of crumpling metal between the La Salle and an elevated pillar. Henderson felt the wheel leap in his hand, and when he got out to investigate saw that the car's running gear was hopelessly bent, the right front wheel toeing in drunkenly. There was nothing to do but wait for a wrecker.

Because his nerves were already worn raw by what had happened that day, the thought of waiting there in the broiling traffic was intolerable to him. So, after identifying himself with the traffic officer on duty and explaining that imperative business called him, he left the La Salle in the policeman's charge and went on.

Thus it was that in the stress of the moment he forgot about his find on the roadside.

When the roadster had been reconditioned, Grey drove it back to Flint's garage, and thought of the narrow chromium band in its pocket slipped yet farther back in the dimness of Henderson's consciousness where it was rapidly buried under an accumulation of other more pressing problems.

XI

MIDWAY through a forenoon three weeks after Norton's funeral, while he was talking to Finley Allen, *Fact's* corpulent literary editor, Henderson's phone rang. Intent on something Allen had just said, he answered it absently.

His brows rose. "Of course. Put her on." To Allen, "It's Julia Norton."

"Hello, Julia," he said into the phone. "Of course. . . . Certainly, I understand. . . . Between four and five this afternoon? Fine. . . . Not at all. . . . Goodbye."

"I'd go with you," Allen said mildly, "only my chastity belt's at the armorer's."

"She wants me to clean Phil's desk out. She hates to ask Hugh to do it."

"I'll bet she does. Well, happy hunting."

Norton's desk yielded little but professional matter. When Henderson had finished, there were, to take to Julia, only a few personal letters, a gold desk-set, Norton's clock, a gold-framed picture of his wife, and a letter tray of odds and ends.

It was nearly five-thirty by the time Henderson was speeding along Northern Parkway toward Oyster Bay. The early evening air was cool and he found himself responding to the quickened colors and scents with a lively pleasure. Even the thought of talking with Julia, which had been irritating that morning, lost its asperity. Henderson had not seen her since Norton's funeral.

He was admitted to the house by a maid he did not recognize and asked to wait in the drawing room. An ormolu clock on the mantel ticked through nearly ten minutes before Julia entered.

"Awfully good of you to do this for me, Baird," she said in a low, carefully controlled voice.

"I was glad to, Julia. There wasn't much except business correspondence."

She crossed to draw the curtains, looked out, and said in surprise, "You've a new car, Baird."

"Like it?"

"A Cord, of all things." She smiled over her shoulder. "It's rather more sporting than I'd have expected."

"I didn't pick it out. It was young Malory's. He needed some cash and so he sold it to me at a bargain."

She frowned. "Malory?"

"Don't you remember the lad who was here the day—?" He broke off. "Protégé of Hugh's. He went back to college a couple of weeks ago."

She smiled suddenly as she drew the curtains and returned to sit on the couch. "I remember. He was terribly concerned about Hugh that day."

"His claque calls him the Future Editor of *Fact.* He's a humorless young ass who takes that seriously. And since he thinks Hugh's in danger, it follows that his own skin——"

"Do you really think Hugh is in danger?"

"No."

For a moment she stared at him intently. Then, "I'm going away for a time, Baird."

"That's wise."

"This place oppresses me. You can understand that? I had to dismiss all the servants. It was—too much like everything going on unchanged to have the same people around."

Henderson nodded.

"Baird," suddenly, "how is Hugh taking this?"

"You know, Julia."

Her lips compressed. "He's under a terrible strain," she said intensely. "Phil's will left all his stock in Fact, Incorporated, to his mother."

Henderson's surprise showed in his face.

"I'm not complaining," Julia went on. "I've enough to get along. But—well, you know Phil's mother. She's a harridan. If she decides she wants to help Hugh run *Fact* . . ." She shrugged.

"She probably won't."

"You can't tell." Then she asked, "Do you think that's all that's bothering Hugh?"

Again Henderson was irritated. "I don't know."

She looked at him sharply. "You think I want to marry Hugh, don't you, Baird?"

Henderson matched her glance. "Don't you?"

"And," she went on, her voice a monotone, her eyes unmoving, *"you think I killed Phil, don't you?"*

Henderson's long face stiffened.

Before he could speak, she said, "Don't lie to me, Baird!"

Henderson said, "I think I'd better be going, Julia."

"I shall be gone some time," Julia said in the same monotone, staring at him. "When I come back, I should hate to find that—people had been talking about me."

"Then," Henderson told her, losing his temper for an instant, "perhaps you'd better not come back, Julia!"

The drive back to the city through the violet night did little to calm the turbulence of his spirit. He felt as if he had been through some disgraceful episode which he could have avoided, and this added a note of self-resentment to his objective anger at Julia Norton. He recalled what Monica had said as they drove away from Flint's country house the night of Norton's death, and his anger increased.

XII

"THE second one I've received," Flint said irritably, "and the blundering incompetents can't find him yet."

Henderson read the letter: "Dear Flint. If you think our account is settled, you are mistaken. I'll have it out with you yet. Do you understand that? And let me warn you not to ruin any more honest businessmen with your fake exposures. Do you understand that, too? You won't find me until I am ready for you to find me, and then I may have an unpleasant surprise for you. George Danisher."

Henderson asked, "Is this what you wanted to see me about?"

"No, Baird. This came in after I called you." Flint stared at the envelope. He put it in his pocket and sat down. "You've been watching the labor trouble developing in the Mesabi country?"

Henderson nodded.

"It looks as though they'll call a strike," Flint continued rapidly. "*Fact* has a lot of basic investments in metal. It would cost us a great deal if those mines were struck."

Henderson, lighting his pipe, looked over the flame, raised his brows.

"I've sent for Lynch Rains," Flint said. "Rains can stop that strike."

Henderson shook out the match. The corners of his mouth drooped. "Do you think he'll come?"

"He *is* coming. He's due now. I wanted you to be here when I talked to him."

"Why?"

Flint made a nervous gesture, started to speak, checked himself. He came around the desk and stood before Henderson. "I've got to depend on you more and more, Baird, now that Phil is gone." For an instant Flint's voice was unsteady. "We've got a great deal ahead of us. You're the only person I can trust to——"

A buzzer sounded. Flint, as if glad to break off the intimacy into which emotion had betrayed him, stepped back, pressed a key, said, "Yes?"

"Mr. Rains to see you, Mr. Flint."

"Have him come in."

The door opened, and Rains was ushered in.

Flint said, "How do you do, Rains?" The words were quick, nervous.

"Hello, Flint." Rains nodded at Henderson. He sat in the chair which Flint indicated. "What is it this time?" he asked calmly. "Has *Fact* changed its mind again?"

"We're seriously considering it, Rains," Flint answered rapidly. "Right now, of course you understand, there is a great deal of confusion and— I want to talk to you about it very soon." He hesitated. "Frankly, Rains, we want to ask a favor of you."

Rains' square face was impassive. It was an awkward moment. The men with whom Flint commonly dealt observed the rules of a tacitly understood game. Rains gave no indication that he knew of the game.

When Flint spoke again, his tone showed that he was nettled at Rains' unwillingness to accept the formality of a cue. "*Fact* has gone out of its way to defend you recently, Rains."

"Defend me? From what?"

"From the innuendoes every newspaper in the country has been printing."

"Innuendoes don't bother me, Flint. They don't bother my men either."

Henderson could see that Flint's temper was shortening momentarily as he realized he was losing control of the interview.

"It might bother those men a good deal if you were accused of Philip Norton's murder," Flint flashed.

Rains looked at him calmly. "You said you had a favor to ask of me."

Flint's lips tightened. His narrow, sharply angled face flexed. "*Fact* has investments in the Mesabi region, Rains," he said shortly. "We don't want a strike there just now."

Again Rains stared at the nervous editor impassively without reply.

"You can stop that strike," Flint challenged.

Rains still said nothing.

"Will you stop that strike?" Flint asked sharply.

Rains said, "No."

There was an instant of unstable silence. "But you admit that you could stop it?"

"I could, yes."

"Proud of that, aren't you, Rains?" Flint's mouth was mocking. "Proud of the whip hand you hold."

"I'm proud of the fact that the men trust me," Rains said evenly. "That was what I was thinking of."

"Trust you to lead them into a strike and on relief ?"

"They won't be on relief. They'll win that strike."

"You mean you'll win it? And because you think you'll win it, you won't listen to a friendly——"

"I won't sell out the men."

"Look here, Rains," Flint broke in. "For God's sake, let's not beat around the bush with pious slogans. We needn't act like a pair of edgy airedales. You and I ought to understand each other."

(Henderson thought, *He's forgotten me entirely*, and smoked his pipe in silence.)

"All right," Rains said. "We ought to understand each other. Do we? I don't think you understand me, Flint. But I think I understand you."

"What do you mean?"

"You've got the Mussolini complex," Rains answered. "You're a big shot, Flint. You like to see people jump when you bark. Most people do jump. You're too big a shot for most people not to jump around when you bark at them. But you want to be still bigger, don't you?"

Flint reddened. "You talk to *me* about a Mussolini complex?" he demanded.

"Don't you like to talk about it?"

"Coming from you, it's damned amusing."

"Why coming from me?"

"Christ, man," Flint burst out, "there isn't another man in the country who's got a fiercer power complex than you have."

"Now that you've asked your favor, was there anything else?"

But Flint was not to be deflected. "You like to think of yourself as a czar, don't you, Rains? Little father to forty million working men! Moses to the lost tribes! Dictator to the masses! You've all the answers, haven't you? All you need is the chance to ram them down our throats."

"And you *have* the chance to ram——"

"What do you mean by that?"

"What is *Fact's* circulation?"

Flint's knuckles on the desk before him whitened. "Did you come here to insult me, Rains?"

"I came because you sent for me—to ask me to do you a favor," Rains said evenly. He studied the angry man across the desk. "Innuendoes still bother *you*, don't they, Flint? When you've been through as many fights as I have, they won't. Only you won't go through as many fights as I have. You won't last that long. You haven't enough to fight *for* to last that long."

Flint's explosive temper burst. He leaped to his feet. "Get out," he said hoarsely. "Get out!"

Rains was also on his feet. His voice, drowning out the other, boomed suddenly in the closed room. "I'll get out, Flint. When I've told you something, I'll get out. When I've told you what a sham you are, you and your pious *Fact.* Pretending to give people the truth, pretending you're too cold and pure and objective to take sides—and knifing us with every word you print. Poisoning the ink you use."

Rains, staring at the sheet-white editor, stopped suddenly. He turned and went out of the office.

For two full minutes Flint stood leaning on his desk, his brilliant eyes fixed on the door through which Rains had gone. Color slowly seeped back into his ashen face.

Henderson, watching him intently, found his own nerves tingling. A scene flashed into his memory: Flint in college leaning on a desk exactly as he was now doing while a political rival taunted him about a defeat, Flint the next instant springing across the desk, his lean fingers at the other's throat. So vivid was the remembered scene that Henderson half rose from his chair, prepared to restrain Flint.

But Flint sank down and sat for another minute looking at the telephone before he picked it up. He said, "Henderson," into the phone in a tight voice, and replaced the phone with a hand that shook.

Henderson, from his chair, said, "At your service."

XIII

A WEEK after Flint's interview with Lynch Rains, *Fact* carried a boxed full-page editorial. Flint himself had written it.

"Why was Philip Norton slain?

"No motive was theft, for a fold containing two hundred dollars in currency remained in his pocket.

"Exhaustive search by score of impartial agencies fails to disclose one personal enmity capable of explaining the obvious passion that impelled the murderer.

"That a simple maniac struck Norton down as he knelt changing a tire is scouted by all competent psychopathologists.

"A final possibility remains.

"Philip Norton was killed by an agency which disapproves of the fearless liberalism of *Fact*.

"Philip Norton was killed by an agency whose way of settling differences is the way of the knout, the firing squad.

"Philip Norton was killed by an agency which

would substitute for the objective, dispassionate interpretation of the facts, a ruthless campaign of terror.

"Philip Norton was a martyr to the cause of freedom of the press.

"Philip Norton fell before the ambition of a Democratyrant.

"That possibility remains."

Henderson, at dinner with Monica Leeds, watched her as she read the editorial. He said, "*Democratyrant* was Hugh's word. He's proud of it."

She asked, "What will Flint do for someone to take Norton's place?"

"Perhaps that's what he has in mind for you."

She made an impatient gesture. "He will probably take full control himself and offer to make you editor of *Fact*, Baird. Will you do it?"

"You're setting me a bad example, turning him down." Then, annoyed with himself for his levity, he said, "I think not."

"Why?"

They faced each other, his unspoken reply sharp and clear as if he had uttered it.

"A publishing business," Monica said thoughtfully, "that puts ideas into the heads of five million people is a powerful little gadget to be under the control of one man."

"What could I do? What could I do about this?" he demanded, indicating the editorial open before her.

"You could do nothing by running away. As editor you might——"

"Bore from within?" He rubbed his cheek and his

eyes glinted humorously at her.

But she refused to be turned. "I overheard some men talking at the Waldorf this noon. They were talking about this article. They took it for granted that Rains killed Norton and that it was only a matter of hours until there would be enough evidence to prove it. They called it terrorism and were quite violent."

"They'd have been violent, anyway," he objected, "whether Flint wrote that or not."

"Perhaps they would. But there are millions of others, small, bewildered businessmen, housewives, professional people—" She leaned toward him intensely. "Those people read *Fact*, Baird. Their speech is shaped by it, and their speech habits shape their thinking. They're restless and discontented, ready to be organized, fused together by an opportunist who can give them flags to wave, lead them in a crusade. We—you and I—must do everything we can to counteract in some fractional way just that sort of thing."

"But you won't take the job Flint wants to give you?"

She looked at him levelly. "No. I won't."

Later, as they drove through Times Square in the leisurely during-theater traffic moving decorously in its broken X under the artificial suns, Henderson sought to maintain himself in its reasuring orderliness as a swimmer, drawn by some irresistible undertow, fights desperately to keep himself within the deceptive smoothness of a surface eddy. But Monica's words kept echoing in his mind, and there came to him, over-poweringly, a feeling of dull futility that often assailed him when he lay awake at night and sensed, beyond the walls of his room, beyond the ramparts of the murmuring city itself, the endless busy maneuverings of the forces of darkness, whose agents were men, bitter men, disillusioned men, men of ambition and cruelty, ceaselessly exploiting the world's travail to enslave other men's minds and souls and crucify their ideals—some on the black crosses and twisted symbols of nationalism, others on minor racks of individual selfishness and malice.

XIV

HENDERSON awoke the next morning, his pulse racing to the urgency of a deep clear overwhelming conviction.

He was in love with Monica Leeds.

By some undecipherable logic, that act had sprung luminously clear as they drove away from the crowded city together the night before. It had been like the opening of some exotic flower whose petals, after a long and secret preparation, suddenly snap from one another and unfold a bloom of rare and exquisite beauty. So sudden was this transformation that it had left Henderson hot, abashed, shy as an adolescent. He had thought, *How simple it would be, had we not known each other so long! How simple it would be if there were not the palpable, impervious past to which this must be carefully fitted!* And, suddenly fearful and confused, he had found, as lovers have from time immemorial, that words were barren and empty things. Yet he had only words. . . .

Chagrin and longing warred within him that day

until he was desperate. Toward the middle of the afternoon as he was on the point of fleeing his office, the door opened and Flint entered.

The weeks which had passed since Norton's murder had marked Flint's sharp, intense face with new wire-fine lines: of grief, of unflinching determination. In an obscure way these lent something of maturity, a fixedness of reference which might have been lacking before. He was quieter these days, less driven by the restlessness that had characterized his unvarying manner before.

"Baird," Flint said, "I've something I've been wanting to say to you."

Henderson waited, unresponsive.

"I've waited," Flint continued, his voice unnaturally low, the words weighted, "to know just where we stood."

He stopped. Henderson still said nothing.

"I know now where we stand," Flint went on, still in the same deliberate tone but with a hint of nascent excitement. "Phil's stock in *Fact*, you know, together with mine constitutes control of the corporation. Phil's stock was left to his mother. I know the terms of his will, and from the moment he died, I've frankly been worried. Mrs. Norton is a strong-willed woman. I didn't know what she might do. But now— I've just come from a conference with her. She has agreed to give me her proxy for the block of stock Phil left her. Do you realize what that means, Baird?"

"The place is yours," Henderson said. There was an edge to the words.

Flint slipped off the desk. He shook his head

sharply. "Not that. It means I can go on with what Phil and I had mapped out for Fact, Incorporated. It means I can carry out the plan he and I were just ready to begin on when . . ." Flint's narrow mouth tightened.

"What plan?"

Red gathered in two pools of excitement in Flint's cheeks. Before he answered, he walked to the window where Henderson stood.

"Look, Baird. Look down there."

"Well?"

"One out of every twelve of those people down there buys our magazine. The other eleven . . ."

"The other eleven don't."

"The other eleven," Flint said, ignoring Henderson's comment, "listen to their radios seven days out of every week. And what do they hear?"

His face was flushed now, his eyes brilliant. He stared down as if hypnotized by the slow shallow stream at the bottom of the narrow canyon.

"They hear tripe," Flint said biting the word impatiently. "Bias, distortion, propaganda."

"That," Henderson agreed, "is a rough approximation."

"Listen," Flint said intensely. "Do you realize, Baird, that we could do the same thing for those people in their radios that we've done with print and paper? We've proved it can be done with print," he rushed on. "We've proved they *want* to know the truth, they *want* to know the facts. We gave them reporting without an ax to grind, told them what was happening, refused to hold out on them, to color what we printed." He struck the window sash.

"And we made history. Five million circulation, Baird. Five million with one magazine! What does that prove? It proves we can give five million what they want every week of the year."

Flint was suddenly hoarse, his voice rising on the mounting tide of his excitement.

Henderson felt an irresistible flicker of enthusiasm answering the other. He fought this down.

"*Now* we can do something so much bigger. . . . Listen, Baird, here is what Phil and I were planning. We're going through with it. *You and I* are going through with it. We're going to make it a monument to Phil. Listen. We'll make more history, Baird. We'll give fifty million listeners *the world*, Baird. Not five million readers, but fifty million listeners. Not canned in a linotype. Not corroded through some moronic commentator, but fresh, raw—*the world* as it turns. Think of it, Baird. Twenty-four hours of living, vital history every day of the year. Wars, tidal waves, revolutions, exploration at the poles, earthquakes, sports, music in Munich, big-game hunting in Kenya, volcanoes in the Pacific—we'll corner it all—by short wave—a hundred high-powered transmitters through the country, operating twenty-four hours a day, there to be heard whenever you wish. We'll *own* it all. Before the big networks think of it."

"You'll need two hundred million dollars."

"A hundred. We can have it. It's waiting for us."

Henderson struggled against the seductive influence of the panorama which Flint's words opened mistily out before him. News—the ultimate modern commodity—news not a day old, not an hour old, but news in the immediacy of its living occurrence. . . . To fend off the tantalus force of the conception, he threw himself suddenly into the midst of Fact, Incorporated. He said, "You've tempted fate, Hugh. You've ridden whirlwinds. You've won. All right. But it's not the kind of victory you can hang up on the wall of a trophy room."

Flint put his hand on Henderson's arm. It was an unaccustomed gesture, sprung from some emotional surge which burst through the man's normal physical barriers.

"Not *I*, Baird. Not Phil and me. *All* three of us. *You* and Phil and I, Baird. I realize that. I've been niggardly about realizing it before." His hand fell from Henderson's sleeve, as his voice suddenly jammed and self-consciousness reasserted itself. "I want you to take Phil's place, Baird," he continued after a moment, softly.

A fierce human cupidity, which he instantly loathed, stormed through Henderson. Norton's place—Norton's salary, a share of *Fact's* cascading profits . . .

He did not realize that the silence between them had lengthened.

"Will you, Baird?" Flint's question was almost humble. It occurred to Henderson how elementally lonely the man was, how inept at the experience of human relations his driving self-centerism rendered him. Again, as on that night on the terrace, the errant sense of responsibility for Flint swept him.

"I'm going to Europe in a week or ten days," Flint went on rapidly. "I'll probably be gone three or four months—working on the organization from a dozen different angles. I'll need someone here to look after things. I want to leave you as editor of *Fact*, Baird."

Henderson said, "I'll have to think it over, Hugh."

Flint's mouth twitched in disappointment. "That means you're—against the plan?"

Henderson said, "Yes." He added, "It's too long a shot."

"It's the logical goal of what we've been building up ever since——"

"But not yet."

"Then when?"

"When you've consolidated. We're in a boom, Hugh."

"We didn't need a boom to start *Fact*."

"We didn't," Henderson agreed. "But we've got one now, Hugh, whether we need it or not. Every poor devil in the publishing business is riding it. *Fact* means to go on after it collapses. We would be insane to mortgage the place to bankers, Hugh."

"We've handled bankers," contemptuously.

"Yes, but bankers are going to be harder and harder to handle. Take my word for it, Hugh. *Fact* has been an investment; like an oil well or a railroad or a mine—something to make money out of. But from now on we'd have to be a tool. The most powerful tool in the world. I don't like the idea of being a tool. Anybody's tool. A banker's tool least of all."

Flint's expression suddenly sharpened. He flashed, "You've talked to— You've talked to Monica Leeds."

Puzzled, Henderson shook his head.

Flint temporized with his eyes. He smiled briefly, covering his confusion. "We'll make the salary six hundred a week and a stock adjustment to cover part of it, if you like."

Henderson, his throat suddenly tight, said, "That's tempting, Hugh, but—" His tongue touched his lips. "I'll have to think about it."

XV

AFTER Flint had left him, Henderson stood for a time looking out across the rooftops and spires of the city, vainly trying to quiet his pounding jubilation.

Indecision still held within him, but he found that his mind was clearer. Pointedly he called Monica, felt the tightness close about his throat as he waited, pulse quickening, for her answer, insisted that he must see her at once. "I know you are," he told her confidently, when she objected that she was in the midst of a hundred imperative details. "But you must see me for a few minutes. . . . Yes, something has happened since I left you, something important. I must talk to you, Monica."

For now, suddenly, it did seem important. He did not examine this anomaly, that what had elicited only a casual response when he faced it at first, standing by the window with Flint thirty minutes before, should now have taken on the proportions of passion.

At first when Henderson entered the room where

Monica sat, her lithe fingers sorting clippings while she dictated to a secretary at her side, the enthusiasm which had lifted him as he came was threatened for an instant. Here, surrounded by responsibilities in which he had no part, insulated from him by an almost palpable aura of success, of fame, she was a different person, and he was suddenly shyer than he had been as they rode together the night before.

He strove to recapture something of the exultant expectancy he had felt, and a measure of it returned to him as he watched her dismiss the secretary.

But instead of saying what was in his heart, he found himself telling her of Flint's offer and his determination to accept it, and he was appalled at the barrenness of what had been bright with meaning a short time before.

"If only you'll come over now, Monica," he ended, his deepset eyes warm and excited, for the eagerness was suddenly flowing full and free again as he saw her smile, "think, darling, what a magnificent time the two of us can have."

"Working for Hugh Flint?"

"Flint can be handled. Flint's not an insuperable obstacle."

Her smile became one-sided. "The very phrase I'd have used to describe him, Baird. An insuperable obstacle to editorial honesty."

He rubbed his cheek and looked at her despairingly. "Does that mean that you won't change your mind, Monica?"

"I won't, Baird."

Unable to sit quietly as a wave of desire washed through him at her casual words, Henderson rose and went to stand by her looking down. She raised her face, the smile still on her lips, the smooth curve of her throat arching.

"Monica," he said, and again, "Monica." His voice was unsteady. "I love you, Monica. I've always hated the idea of your accepting Flint's offer, I mean, it always seemed like a bribe. But this afternoon—this afternoon it was suddenly a glorious prospect." He stopped, miserable at once because he knew what she must be thinking. "I know. I've been a shoddy sort, Monica. I've been jealous of you. A part of me that's selfish and mean has been jealous of your success, of the things you can do, the name you have." Again he broke off as the turbulence of love and remorse and hope and fear jammed in the narrowness of his words and overpowered him. "I love you," he said in a whisper, his hands on her hands, his eyes pleading.

Then he was drawing her up into his arms, and because she did not resist, the room whirled about them.

At last she pushed him away and laughed into his eyes. "You've been a very long time, Baird dear, a very long time. I had begun to be afraid you'd be forever."

"Please, Monica," he said, "won't you change your mind?" Remembering, he continued eagerly, "Flint's going abroad in a week or two for several months. You and I could——"

"Begin to undo what *Fact* may be doing to Lynch Rains?"

He scarcely heard her. "That. A thousand things. Between us, darling."

She laid her hand on his and her mouth was smiling, though there was a curious expression in her gray-green eyes. "You've got a magnificent enthusiasm, Baird dear, and I suspect you've lousy control of it. I'd much rather go somewhere and have a drink and celebrate than talk about *Fact* just now."

XVI

LYNCH RAINS was indicted exactly one month after Norton's funeral. Over the hot protests of the local prosecutor, he was admitted to bail of $20,000 and released at dusk to walk from the courthouse into a barrage of flashing bulbs and clicking news cameras.

Deliberate, impassive, he strode through the newsmen flanked by his lawyers, frowned at the blinding blooms of the flash bulbs, shook his head at requests of the reporters. A solid chunk of man, impervious, untouched by the confusion of which he was focus.

Henderson, sitting with Flint in Flint's maroon Cadillac opposite the courthouse, looked at the silent man at the wheel.

He saw Flint's fingers tighten on the wheel, saw the muscles at the corner of his mouth twitch. Just before Rains reached the sedan waiting for him, he looked across the street and saw Flint.

Henderson felt the editor stiffen.

Then Rains had broken away from the group

surrounding him and was coming across the street. The reporters, alert for drama, recognizing that Rains was making for Flint's car and aware that conflict was in the air, straggled after him, photographers awkwardly changing bulbs and plates as they ran down from the courthouse lawn.

An avid semicircle formed behind Rains as he halted, facing Flint.

"You've got your holy war, haven't you, Flint?" Rains asked. He paused for the space of a knife-thrust. "Don't let your mania for the truth stop you."

Then, pushing aside the newspapermen who would have detained him and prolonged the scene, he went back across the street, got in beside his two lawyers, and was driven away.

XVII

FLINT started the motor. They hurtled forward. Then as the flush ebbed from his narrow face, and his hands on the wheel slowly relaxed their tension, he moved his shoulders and settled back into the corner of the leather-cushioned seat, as if the turbulence in him flowed out now into the encompassing, effortless rhythm of the droning engine.

His mouth twitched. "Iscariot!"

Henderson, puzzled, asked, "Iscariot?"

Flint drew a breath. "A *worse*, Baird." His tone, like his attitude, was drained of passion, rational. "Judas betrayed only one man. Rains—men like him—he the most dangerous—is doing his best to betray millions."

"How betray?"

"Planting hatreds where no hatreds are."

"But where the soil is ripe for hatreds?"

Flint looked aside at Henderson. In his narrow face lay repose. His eyes were cool; their expression as he caught Henderson's glance was reproachful.

The September evening was lowering and chill. Rain hung in the dragging, dirty clouds. Flint shivered suddenly and raised the window at his shoulder, reaching forward to the heater switch.

A traffic light stopped them at a deserted corner. The wind whipped a sudden spray of rain against the windshield. Flint's hands grew restless on the wheel; he raced the motor impatiently. He did not speak until they were moving again.

"Very few plain men want wealth. That is where men of wealth are misled by an illusion. What do most plain men want? What does the man with the dinner pail want? Strikes? Conflict?" Flint shook his head. "He wants security, Baird. If necessary, he is willing to fight to wrest that from the small minority of selfish men among the owners of industry. But Rains is not content to right *actual* abuses. Momentum, ambition for power, carries him on. And it carries after him all those who, because they are bewildered, listen to him in their bewilderment."

"Bewilderment can spring from empty bellies."

"Then the bellies must be filled, Baird."

"Splendid," Henderson said. His tone was caustic. "Suppose we devote the magnificent resources of Fact, Incorporated, to that end."

The other looked at him. Like all passionately self-centered men, Henderson reflected, Flint was slow to kindle to sarcasm. This gave him a sense of strength as when, facing an encounter with an opponent whose skill he knows well enough not to underrate, a man feels a new weapon surreptitiously slipped into his hand.

"When we've finished with Rains," Flint said,

"perhaps we will."

XVIII

THERE was a peculiar intensity to the excitement inspired by Rains' indictment. In a land where news is an ornamented commodity, some amount of fanfare is certain to accompany criminal proceedings against any man much in the public eye, but the case of the State vs. Lynch Rains produced something more.

Henderson was conscious of this as he read headlines in metropolitan papers, as his sardonic eye skimmed hinterland editorials whose writers snowed clippings on *Fact* in ever increasing volume, as he listened to conversations in which, more and more reluctantly, he was led to participate.

Periodically he was reminded of Rains' bitter comment: "You've got your holy war, haven't you, Flint?" At first this was merely an annoyance, but as incidents capable of snapping the phrase back into his mind occurred with greater frequence, he found himself beginning to respond angrily, trying to blur the scene in his memory and succeeding only in refreshing it to the point of photographic clarity.

He recalled the violent undertow of hatred which had dragged at Flint's words as they drove away from the courthouse together, and he was sensible that the unreason of that hatred was spreading, widening, becoming, as the days passed and then weeks, a strong tide sweeping Rains inexorably toward a fate already taken for granted by hordes of *Fact* readers. Their letters flooded mail pouches and sorting tables, a thin stream of protest lost in the loud sure clamor of approval of *Fact's* campaign for the conviction of a man accused of murdering an editor who had been a name and was now a symbol.

"*Fact's* campaign!" Henderson burst out to Monica one night. "*Fact's* campaign! Great God, there hasn't been a colored line on Rains for four weeks."

"Flint's editorial——"

"That was two months ago. Flint's been out of the country since the tenth."

When she did not speak, Henderson's irritation sharpened. "*Fact's* campaign!" he repeated savagely. "*Fact's* fearless stand . . . *Fact's* uncompromising war on terrorism . . . *Fact's* unflinching defense of all that Democracy holds dear . . ."

"Sterling phrases."

Henderson grunted. "Two thousand letters this week—every one hurling Bartlett's *Familiar Quotations* at me."

She was silent again. They were riding up Fifth Avenue toward the theater district. Their cab had been halted by a red light at Forty-first Street, and the hush which surrounded them in the all but empty Avenue seemed a projection of Monica's own silence. Henderson, looking up at the dimly lighted portico of the Library, resented the silence.

Monica asked, "Why did Flint go abroad?"

"Business," shortly.

"Oh."

He looked at her. "Why do you have to be so difficult, dear?" he complained. "I'm tired, Monica. I'm hellishly tired. Can't I get away from it—even with you?" He took her hand.

She asked quietly, "Can you?"

They were on the point of turning west into Forty-third Street when Henderson leaned forward suddenly and said to the driver, "Go on to the Park." He sat back and said grimly, "1 don't feel like the season's smash comedy."

"I want to ask you something, Baird," Monica said after a time.

"Yes?"

"What do you know about Julia Norton?"

"I think I told you once."

She said slowly, "Julia was involved with two men on the night of the murder, do you remember?"

"A third she put to bed with a migraine headache."

Monica threw a quick glance at him, was on the point of saying something, checked herself, and after a moment went on, "I've found out something about Flint's chauffeur, Grey."

"What?"

"He used to work for one of the men Hugh Flint

visited in England about a year ago. This gentle-
man's wife seems to have been a frail vessel and
Grey— Anyway, Hugh Flint took a liking to him. A
passport and an immigration permit were fixed up
for him, and Flint brought him back to the States
last April."

"You've gone to a lot of trouble."

"It wasn't hard. I began thinking after it occurred to us that whoever was on that side of the
house should have seen Norton's car stop in the
lane. I began with the immigration records. A lad I
know on the Manchester *Guardian* did the rest."

"Interesting as biography. The relevance escapes
me."

He saw a twitch of annoyance at the corner of
her lips.

She said quietly, "Grey was having an affair with
Julia Norton when her husband was killed."

"What newspaperman found that out for you,
darling?"

"It was chiefly intuition. You needn't look too
closely at that female chassis," swift scorn in her
words, "to conclude she wouldn't spend her time
with a handsome chauffeur just gossiping about
London. Flint's cook verified it for me."

Henderson laughed. "My dear! Backstairs in-
trigue."

This time the annoyance that tightened her
mouth lingered in her eyes as she looked at him. "A
man will soon be on trial for his life before what will
probably be a hostile jury. Some of the rules are
suspended at a time like this, Baird."

A guilty sense of having been remiss stung Henderson. It was more than a passing flick. Shame and a feeling of personal perfidy assailed him as he remembered how hot his blood had run immediately after the murder. This intensified his persistent weariness and irritation, and with an effort he kept his voice calm as he asked, "Why are you so interested in Rains, Monica?"

She hesitated, looking out the window at the filigree of towered lights far across the Park meadow. At last she turned to him, and now her eyes were alight with anger. "You wouldn't have asked me that a month ago, Baird."

XIX

IT had not been a quarrel. There had been no open clash, no unguarded flare of bitterness. The very restraint that held between them as they rode back downtown to Monica's apartment, where he left her, was the more distressing to Henderson for that reason. Looking back on it, as he lay sleepless, panic caught at him that they should have parted thus, almost without words, under the eyes of a cab driver and a doorman.

And because his thoughts circled back inexorably to the thing that had come between them, he could not escape the pressure of a hateful futility.

If Rains were really not guilty . . . If the man were telling the truth . . . A sudden animal fright swept Henderson, chilling him, shocking him into tense, harsh wakefulness. For an instant, so vivid was the experience, he seemed himself to sense with an immediacy transcending logic the sheer brute threat of death—the threat which, no matter how strong the man might be, must lie with Lynch Rains day in and day out, hour for hour, as his trial neared.

But what could he do for Rains? What that the law itself, with the infinitely specialized means at his beck, could not do? It was absurd of Monica to tax him with neglect. A man had been killed. Another man now stood in danger of his life. It was for the law to determine. Must he turn melodramatic hero of a tinsel plot, rush about cunningly piecing together clues which the police failed to see?

Yet he could not completely exorcize the shade of that momentary vicarious menace which had seized him, and it was with relief like the snapping of a spring that he saw by the headline on his paper next morning that Rains' trial had been postponed. Saul Kaufman, wily chief of Rains' defense staff, had secured a change of venue, arguing that a power strike in the county seat had created a prejudicial atmosphere. The trial was now set for the first week of January in New York County.

Henderson called Monica at once. Yes, she had heard. They talked for a moment, and he hung up with a dull return of the despair which had visited him the night before. It occurred to him that what appeared to be a minor victory for Rains could be interpreted in an entirely different light. Would Saul Kaufman, brilliant strategist, resort to such clumsy tactics as this unless he himself were convinced that his client's case was indeed desperate?

The despair which had tightened within him as he broke off his brief conversation with Monica grew unbearable. He knew an imperative desire to talk to her face to face, to grope back toward that whole, warm, lively sympathy they had enjoyed in each other before last night.

Leaving word with his secretary that he might not return that day, Henderson left the building and ten minutes later was standing on a floor occupied by National Features, his hand on the knob of a door which bore "Miss Leeds" in small block letters. He looked at the name, and its impersonal professional stamp checked the impulsive assurance which had grown in him as he walked briskly across town in the late October chill. Once more he was suddenly humble and uncertain of himself.

He opened the door.

The man sitting across the desk from Monica was Lynch Rains.

Henderson stopped short.

Monica looked toward him. "Oh, Baird. Come in. You know Mr. Henderson, I believe, Mr. Rains?"

Rains nodded. "Hello, Henderson."

Henderson, obscurely nettled as if some trick had been played on him, said, "I didn't know you were busy. I'll come back later, Monica."

"Come in."

Henderson entered and sat down.

He looked at Rains, saw the changes which the weeks had wrought. The man's face, like his hands and shoes, like his chunk of torso, was square, solid; in it laughter had etched no lines, yet before this it had not been the face of a man who could not laugh. There was still power in the jut of a chin beneath a mouth to which words would come deliberately, in the short pugnacious nose, the square forehead. There was still a strong independence in Rains' steady black eyes. But the solidity and strength were rather now the surface show of a mass at whose core a corrosive acid had been at work. Rains' mouth was that of a man harassed by unremitting strain.

Monica was explaining that she planned a series of articles on industrial conditions and had asked Rains to come in and discuss a schedule of approach.

"You can tell Flint," Rains said, his black eyes flashing at Henderson, his voice resonantly ironic, "that I'm not doing anything for Miss Leeds directly. Flint probably wouldn't like that."

Henderson said nothing.

"I'm going to begin," Monica said, "with a trip to Mifflin."

"*Fact* hasn't had much to say about Mifflin lately," Rains observed. "Is Flint too busy with his holy war?"

"Flint is in Europe," Henderson said shortly. Then he asked, "Do you want to know why *Fact* hasn't had much to say about Mifflin, Rains?"

"Why?"

"Because I've killed five stories myself."

"Fact stories?"

Henderson's lean face colored. He asked, "Are you afraid of factual stories? Is that what you mean?"

"Did you think you were doing us a favor by keeping mention of Mifflin out of *Fact*, Henderson?"

"Not particularly. I didn't like the facts myself."

"Oh, you didn't?"

"I didn't," Henderson said, battening down his temper. "I disliked them as much as you do, Rains."

"And because I dislike them the same way," Monica added, "I intend to print something about them."

Rains and she continued to talk for a few minutes, finishing the interview which Henderson had interrupted. He grew more and more uncomfortable, aware that his pettish outburst must have alienated her once more as surely as had his manner of the night before. Furious with himself, he tried to understand how he had been betrayed into speaking thus, and was uneasy when he could not. He knew only that there would be no opportunity now to do what he had come for, and he was rebellious.

At length he rose, gave a stiff apology, and left. Monica made no attempt to dissuade him from going.

The door closed slowly behind him, so slowly that, as he hesitated an instant and looked back, he caught a sharp picture of Lynch Rains silhouetted against the window, his strong profile betrayed by that telltale defenseless sagging beneath the chin.

It was to be the last glimpse of Rains he would have for many weeks. An hour later, his bail having been revoked, Rains was rearrested and jailed at the behest of the prosecutor, who claimed to have discovered his plans to leave the country on a forged passport.

Forged passports being much in the news just then, this caused a sensation and created a fresh outburst of diatribes.

Saul Kaufman withdrew from the defense the

following day, arid this was widely recognized as evidence of the hopelessness of Rains' case.

Hugh Flint, in Berlin, sent a gratulatory cable to the member of the prosecution staff credited with having unearthed Rains' plot to flee.

XX

NOVEMBER and early December passed in a welter of fuming detail. Henderson still found his new responsibilities chaotic and maddening, their complexity and grim unrelenting pressure threatening now and then to overwhelm him.

Matters were not improved by the fact that a slow but ominous recession from the peak which industrial tempo had reached was apparent throughout the business world. Advertising accounts were to be held only at the cost of constantly increasing pressure on the part of the promotion department, whose members Henderson drove as unrelentingly as he himself was driven; newsstand sales showed a dangerous slackening; and, despite the redoubled efforts of specialized subscription divisions, subscribers had begun dropping like the nervous leaves of autumn as October merged into November and November became December.

During the holidays Clark Malory appeared on the scene to continue his apprenticeship. Henderson, cursing Flint and his guild affectations *in absentia*, set the youth to indexing. He was forced to admit, however, that Clark had improved. Indeed, The Future Editor of *Fact* rasped Henderson's nerves so little that on the fourth night as they waited for the elevator together and Henderson realized that he had actually forgotten about Clark's presence, an oblique sense of contrition caused him suddenly to invite the lad to dinner.

He had no occasion at first to regret this magnanimity. The boy was amiable and entertaining as he described the success he was having with his campus magazine, mentioned problems which paralleled those of the parent *Fact*.

"By the way," he said, and the eagerness in his voice was genuine, "I'd like awfully to see Miss Leeds again, Henderson. I know she thinks I'm a cub, but—I mean I think she's magnificent. She's too good for National Features. I don't see why she stays there."

Henderson found himself looking forward to the evening. He would draw this youngster out, discover his possibilities, perhaps even counteract in some elementary fashion the spoiling Flint was fostering.

But Clark's next words made Henderson quench this missionary glow.

"I suppose you don't know why Flint is in Europe, Henderson." (It was the tone chiefly—condescending, patronizing.)

"I think I do, yes."

"Oh." Then after an interval, "I didn't know he wanted it publicly known yet."

"He doesn't," Henderson said dryly.

"I knew about it, of course, last summer."

"Did you?"

"I probably wasn't supposed to, of course. But, you know, placed as I was last summer——"

"Yes," Henderson agreed, "placed as you were."

"—I couldn't help knowing about a great many things."

"I suppose not."

"I'm glad Flint got things straightened out so he could go ahead with *Fact-On-The-Air.*"

Henderson, staring wearily out the window at the surging shoppers engulfing them at a corner, said absently, "Yes." Then he frowned. He looked at Clark. "Straightened out?"

The youth flushed, and as Henderson held his eyes they grew uncomfortable. "You know what I mean."

"What?"

There was a pause. "You honestly don't know?" Clark asked.

"Don't know what?"

"About Norton, I mean," Clark said.

Henderson said, "Oh, of course," and stared out the window, waiting.

"About how Norton was trying to wreck everything."

"Oh now, not everything."

"He tried to play hell with *Fact-OnThe-Air,* didn't he?"

Henderson said evenly, "I didn't know you knew about that."

"There were mighty few things I didn't know."

Clark shrugged. "What's the use of talking about it? Flint's going ahead now. I can tell from what he said in the letter I got last week that everything's coming along."

They did not recur to the subject. Henderson, after the first rush of surprise had passed, took himself sharply to task for succumbing to Clark's egoist fabrication and (until he grew ashamed of the sport) spent their dinner hour leading Clark on to inflate his adolescent ego.

As he watched Clark, Henderson was impressed with the likeness between the boy and Flint. It was as if, by some chronological alchemy, he were suddenly permitted from his adult vantage to look back through the crowded years and see Flint as Flint himself had been when a senior in college.

The pattern of similarity between the youth and Flint continued to clarify. Toward the end of the meal it leaped into shocking relief. A waiter, bending over young Malory's shoulder, let his tray slip. A bowl of French dressing slid, spilled down Clark's sleeve.

The boy leaped up, his eyes furious. "You clumsy fool!"

Instead of apologizing, the waiter chose (gallantly, Henderson thought) not to truckle. "What're you going to do about it?" he demanded.

Clark Malory gasped. Then, before Henderson could leap up and stop him, he had plunged across the table.

It took but an instant for Henderson to throw the youth back onto the leather bench, but even in that instant there leaped before his inward eye the picture of Flint springing across a desk at a long-forgotten political rival—the picture that had flashed into his memory on the day Lynch Rains had turned contemptuously on his heel and walked out of Flint's office.

"Another episode like this," Henderson promised grimly as he escorted the youth out of the restaurant, "and I'll personally tear up that contract."

XXI

HENDERSON did not see Flint the day the other returned from abroad. The next afternoon Flint came into Henderson's office, his sharp, nervous eyes alight with interest. His greeting was rapid, merely a brief prelude to an excited, "Did you see Monica Leeds' column on the Rome-Berlin axis this morning? I was never more right in my life," he continued enthusiastically, "than when I realized that girl could do the job we want done. Look, Baird, your word has some weight with her. Can't you persuade her?"

Henderson, surprised, for he had fully expected Flint to burst out with a comment on Rains, shook his head. "I've my hands full."

There was a moment of silence.

Flint said, "Another of those letters came today. Another letter from Danisher."

"What did he say?" (Could Danisher be the answer to Lynch Rains' tragic puzzle after all?)

"Wild, incoherent threats like the others. It was mailed from upstate." Flint's mouth hardened. His fingers flicked as if he were dismissing the topic with the gesture.

Henderson could see that he was already thinking of something else. A moment later he went out of Henderson's room.

He had not once mentioned Rains. This shocked Henderson. Was it Rains Flint had been thinking of? Yet he had not spoken Rains' name. It was unthinkable that Rains had not been in his mind. Norton's death was too close to both of them for them to greet each other thus after a separation, on the eve of Rains' trial, without tacitly reminding each other.

Flint's refusal to talk of Rains seemed to Henderson ominous beyond any reason he could assign to it. The feeling persisted. Twice later he talked to Flint that day and not once did Flint speak of the trial, not once did he mention Rains.

Toward four o'clock Henderson answered the telephone and heard Clark Malory ask if he might come in. Henderson's mind leaped to what Clark had said a fortnight before. Something within him moved in a quick jerk of suspicion which he realized he had never until that moment actually allowed to mature. Yet now, with Flint's inexplicable silence clouding the atmosphere about him . . .

Malory's eyes behind their octagon lenses were oddly anxious as he stood before Henderson.

"What is it, Clark?"

It came to him that the only other time he had seen the boy so moved was on the day they had ridden together to the inquest and Clark had expressed his fears for Flint's safety. For a reason

which he angrily refused to recognize, this coinci-
dence gave Henderson a chill prescience.

"I'd appreciate it, Henderson——"

"Yes?"

"I mean you won't mention anything to Mr. Flint
about what I said the other night, will you, Henderson?"

"Why not?"

Clark flushed, his eyes defensive. "I wouldn't
want him to know I'd been a snotty little gossip," he
said, the words unexpectedly humble.

Henderson started to speak, checked himself. He
looked at Clark steadily. The boy's eyes returning
the gaze, hardened once more; the flush left his
face.

"All right, Clark. I'll say nothing to Hugh——"

"Thanks," quickly.

"On one condition."

"What?" The question was eager. "If you'll tell me
the truth."

"Of course. What, Henderson?"

"How long had you known about *Fact-On-The-Air*
last summer?"

"How long?"

"How long."

"How long before what, Henderson?"

"Before Norton was killed."

"A couple of weeks."

Henderson's next question was casual. "How
long had you known that Norton opposed the idea?"

"Don't you see, Henderson," the boy answered
swiftly, his voice strained again, the anxious light
reappearing in his eyes, "that's what I mean. About

being a snotty little gossip."

"It wasn't true, then?"

"I was making it up, Henderson. By the yard," miserably.

"Why?"

"God knows."

"Did Flint ever say anything to give you the basis for that lie?" Henderson demanded, suddenly thoughtless of caution.

Clark's eyes were frightened. He shook his head. "Not a thing, Henderson, not a thing. Christ, but I was a fool to say a thing like that. I ought to be booted out of *Fact* on my tail for saying what I said that night. I thought I had to have something to talk to you about. I wanted to impress you." He broke off. "You won't say anything to Mr. Flint?" he pleaded.

Henderson had never before seen him abject.

"All right, Clark. I'll say nothing to Hugh. We'll forget it."

"Thanks. Thanks a lot. He'd think I was a——"

"Very well. Only don't have any more delusions."

"I won't," fervently. Then again, "Thanks, Henderson."

When the boy had gone, Henderson tried to work, but the swelling grain of perfectly specific suspicion prevented him from concentrating. He was on the point of calling Monica, when chagrin and inverted rebellion prevented. During the six weeks since he had sat in her office with Lynch Rains they had seen each other seldom. The day after Rains' arrest Monica had taxed him with his behavior, and Henderson had been sufficiently nettled to answer in peevish words; they had quarreled. The memory of that quarrel was bitter to Henderson, as bitter as the longing which drew him at every thought of her. But stubbornness and a certain awkwardness kept him from the reconciliation which he was unsure how to effect.

Now as he thought of what Clark had said, he longed to talk to her, to share with her his slowly unfolding, incredible suspicion. He thought to himself, "Rains' trial is but a week away," and the words startled him. He must find something, must pierce through to some stable, solid certainty. It was urgent.

XXII

SELECTION of a jury to try Rains began the following Thursday and proceeded through Friday and Saturday.

At eleven o'clock Monday forenoon, Henderson was buying tobacco in a cigar store when the radio, which had just chimed softly, broke into rapid speech.

"We interrupt the next program to bring you a special bulletin from the Press Radio Bureau. New York: The jury which will try Lynch Rains, labor leader, for the murder last August of Philip Norton, wealthy North Shore publisher, was completed a few minutes ago. The trial, which through a change in venue, is being held in New York County, will open tomorrow with the prosecution's presentation of its case. That the death penalty will be demanded was clear from the beginning of the jury selection, the prosecution rejecting every prospective juror who admitted a prejudice against capital punishment. A summary of the first session of the trial will be brought to you at twelve-fifteen Eastern Standard Time tomorrow afternoon over the station to which you are now listening. We take you now to Chicago where . . ."

The tobacconist, handing Henderson's change to him, nodded with relish. "They'll fry that guy."

Henderson went out of the store, the man's words with their overtone of indifferent hatred clogging his mind.

He had scarcely reached the office when Flint telephoned, his voice buoyant with excitement.

"Get Monica Leeds and have her meet us in your office at five," Flint said. "We'll go out for cocktails and on to dinner and a show. Don't worry about clothes. I won't have time to dress. I've got something to tell you both."

Henderson's mouth was wry as he replaced the phone. How like Flint to arrange an affair thus abstractly with no thought but that the pawns would shift docilely into their places. He was glad, however, of this objective opportunity to arrange a meeting with Monica, aware of a certain feeling of relief that they would not be alone. Perhaps something would happen; perhaps he could make something happen to close the rift between them.

His throat was tight, the blood hot in his temples, as he called her. He fumbled with the question, incredulity sweeping him when she agreed readily.

Eagerly he turned to his work in order to speed the day's hours until he would see her.

As usual, his routine was filled with nagging problems that raced without respite on each other's heels, overlapped, snarled into jammed crises, un-

til, shortly before five when he told his secretary to
go, it was mere animal fatigue that drove him from
his desk to stand in the window and stare out at
the early dark dropping over the city.

There was a rap at his door. He wheeled.

Julia Norton said calmly, "Hello, Baird."

She came into the room and shut the door. She
was slimmer, tanned, her selfish, dissatisfied
mouth quieter, her eyes level and empty of the passion he had seen flame in them that afternoon three
months before.

She looked around the room to which the au-
thentic note of luxury still clung. "Um. Come up in
the world, haven't you, Baird?"

"Away up," he agreed, an eyebrow slanting. "How
long have you been back, Julia?"

"Last night. Missed me, haven't you, Baird?" She
made a provocative mouth at him and laughed.
"Still the same old Baird, isn't it? What's happened
on the home front?"

"Not a great deal."

"Don't stall, Baird. I've been the hell and gone to
Honolulu. I haven't seen a paper for months. Did
they convict Rains?"

Henderson, aware that she was lying, tried to
read her eyes. Under his scrutiny they grew arrogant, opaque as agates.

"There was a power strike in Mineola. His lawyers got a change of venue." He nodded. "That's
why you're back."

"I'm back because I got good and ready to come
back. How's Hugh?"

"Chiefly invisible."

She raised penciled brows. Then she chuckled. "Still the good shepherd, aren't you, Baird? Has the girl wonder got him hooked yet?"

Henderson frowned.

"Don't be YMCA, Baird," she said petulantly. Then, "I hear she's still coy at the idea of working for *Fact*."

"So you haven't been entirely out of touch."

Julia chuckled again. "Do you think I'm going to sit back and let that glittering intellect——"

"You needn't worry."

She frowned. Then light dawned in her eyes. She said, "Well, well, well, isn't that definitely?" She laughed. "Anyway, Baird, I'm not worried. About Hugh, I mean. Just the maternal instinct. Hugh would be putty in the Leeds hands."

She took out a cigarette case, lighted a cigarette, held the open case to him, and put it away when he shook his head.

"Baird," she said thickly, squinting at him seriously through the drifting smoke, "don't you know that girl is ambitious? Don't you see that she's using you? That she's using Hugh, that she won't be satisfied until she's climbed on all your shoulders, especially Hugh's? She's reaching for the sky, Baird. And to climb up on Hugh's shoulders to do that, she'll have to marry him." She made a petulant gesture with her cigarette. "It's the only way she can make sure of controlling him. My God, you were ready to believe it about me when——"

The door opened quickly. Monica Leeds started in, checked herself, "Sorry, Baird. I didn't know——"

Julia turned, smiled, "Hello. Come in. We were

just talking about you."

"Mrs. Norton. I didn't recognize you."

"It's the surf," Julia said candidly. "Does things to your hips and ankles." She rose. "If you want to get in touch with me, Baird, I'm staying in town." She smiled from him to Monica, and mentioned a telephone number. Then she went out.

"So the passion flower is with us again," Monica observed.

She dropped into a chair, throwing open her trim camel's-hair coat, its fur hiding all but the curve of her cheek for an instant as she turned to look at a book on the low table beside her, the smart brown hat, peaked, arrogantly new-season, even the stitching on her modish gloves as her slim hand curved to open the book's cover—swift details to which Henderson would normally have been blind now suddenly invested with the sharpness of longing . . .

He went to her, stood before her. She looked up, smiled. Suddenly he caught her and drew her up to him as he had that first day, seeking through the impersonal stuff of her gloves for contact with her hands, his eyes hot as he compelled her to look at him.

He laughed deep in his throat, bent to kiss her, and it was as if an insupportable burden slipped from him. He held her away from him, said lightly, for he was fearful of losing this buoyant relief by recognizing it in words, "She thinks you're angling for Hugh. She's concerned about it."

"How stupid. What did she say?"

"She pretended to know nothing about the trial.

Talked of your pathological ambition, darling."

Monica flushed angrily and drew away from him. This unaccustomed reaction surprised Henderson. Impulsive wrath was foreign to her, that instant display about her eyes and mouth incongruous as heat lightning against the January sky.

"Did she say I wanted to use Flint?"

"Something of the sort. Flint and me, dearest." He smiled at her. "She probably expects to make better headway with Hugh herself now. She's come back for that, of course."

"You think so, Baird?"

"She'll make a fetching witness for the prosecution, of course."

Monica frowned. She asked, "Has it occurred to you that you might make a fitting candidate in more than one line of succession?"

Henderson's mouth opened. Then he laughed heartily. He took her by the arms. "My darling Cassandra. Eve sleeps close to the surface, what?"

An instant after he had released her, the door opened. Hugh Flint came in quickly. "Oh, hello, Miss Leeds. Waiting long?"

Flint's narrow face was red, his eyes bright with a wrath apparently so recent it was still at white heat.

Henderson thought, *Julia went to him from here, of course*. This shocked him, sobered him, recalled the gravity of the suspicion which had wormed into his consciousness, reawakened in him the sense of bitter obligation.

XXIII

DURING dinner Flint was nervous and talkative, his sharp, uneasy eyes bright with some barely restrained climactic emotion, its announcement trembling time after time behind a staccato rush of conversation. He had not yet come to the point, however, when they left the restaurant and went on to *Hooray for What!*

Here Henderson found the thought of Lynch Rains intruding constantly, maddeningly, between him and Ed Wynn's clowning. He tried to shake himself free from this mood, tried to be conscious of nothing but the sweetness of Monica's shoulder against his own—and was rasped by the sound of Flint's laughter.

After the play, as they stood on the sidewalk, Henderson, glancing down at the morning editions displayed by a curb newsboy, saw "Chair for Lynch?" in blatant type, a picture of the imprisoned man staring up from the page at him. The picture had apparently been snapped that day as Rains was taken from the courtroom. It was the face of an old man, almost unrecognizably changed since Henderson had last seen Rains only seven weeks before.

Flint's voice broke in. "Splendid. Awfully nice of you. How about it, Baird?"

He asked, startled, "What?"

"I suggested that we go down to my apartment and scramble eggs," Monica said.

An hour later Henderson, leaning lazily against the mantelpiece, watched Monica, his eyes troubled, and thought of the picture which had stared accusingly up at him from the sidewalk. Flint was talking, and the suddenly heightened excitement in his voice intruded on Henderson's frustration.

"Slavery? What slavery is there worse than men's building an idolatry out of their own worst vices? That, we must prevent here at all costs. It is the duty of people like ourselves to prevent it, Miss Leeds."

As if he could restrain himself no longer, Flint was on his feet, looking down at Monica, his eyes bright, intense. "For any intelligent writer to shirk that duty today is treason—treason to the traditions which have molded his intelligence." He caught himself abruptly, and then rushed on, the words rapid, explosive. "*Fact* recognizes that duty, Miss Leeds. Every writer for *Fact* is aware of it. You yourself recognize that duty. You indicate it in your work. Yet you have consistently refused to come in with us, to join forces with us." He paused, his eyes glittering. "You can't refuse longer, Miss Leeds."

Henderson, puzzled, stared at the man whose voice shook as he spoke.

Monica asked sharply, "What do you mean?"

Flint said, the words tumbling, "In a very short time, *Fact* is going on the air, Miss Leeds. On the air with a plan that will revolutionize radio. We'll bring history-in-the-making into every home in the land. Not pallidly dramatized as *Time* does. History itself! Living, raw, history-in-the-act. From key senders of our own in the world's turbulent spots, through our own short-wave facilities, our own broadcasting stations here in America. Our audience—your audience, Miss Leeds, will be the entire radio public."

"My audience?"

But Flint was not to be swerved in the swift tide of his enthusiasm. *"Fact* has gone as far as a publication with national circulation can go in reporting immediate news. There is now a minimum of lag between event and presentation. But that minimum of lag will always remain where the medium is the printed word. Radio is the solution! News by radio will require no more than minutes of editing and transmission. Under the present handicap, even *Fact's* writers must be at least four days from their readers." Flint broke off. "We will begin broadcasting five weeks from tomorrow. You, Miss Leeds, will be women's editor of *Fact-On-The-Air!"*

"Why do you say that?"

"As a writer for National Features Syndicate," Flint said, triumph hot in his words, "you are to-night a part of Fact, incorporated."

There was a taut, unstable silence. "What do you mean?"

"We've had an interest in National Features for

some time," Flint said. "This afternoon that interest became a controlling one. As soon as present contracts run out, Miss Leeds, your column will be restricted to *Fact.*"

In the moment of silence that followed, Flint sank into a chair, sat there tensely.

Monica rose, walked to the radio murmuring in a corner of the room. She shut the instrument off and came back. Still standing, facing Flint, she said, her voice trembling, "If I have been, as you say, a member of Fact, Incorporated, since this afternoon, I can only apologize. I am giving you my resignation now. You will have it confirmed in writing in the morning."

Flint's eyes flashed. He straightened. "What?"

"I will not work for *Fact.* Do you want to know why? Because, in my opinion, you have made it a combination of the worst features of newspaper immediacy and magazine license. That is why. Your lust for immediacy leaves no room for honest interpretation. *Fact-On-The-Air* is the logical product of that lust. It appalls me."

Henderson looked at Flint. His face was granitic, only his burning eyes marking the wrath which Monica's words had whipped high.

When Flint spoke, his voice was unrecognizable. "Are you coming, Baird?"

Henderson said, "Not yet."

When Flint had gone, and the silence between the two of them had lengthened out, Henderson went to sit on the arm of Monica's chair. He took her shoulders, but instead of responding, she was rigid a moment, and then pushed him away to get up and walk toward the fire.

"Need you let it stand between us?" he asked.

She leaned against the mantel and touched an andiron with her toe. "I can't divide myself into logic-tight sections that easily, Baird."

"You think I should resign, too?"

"You may do exactly as you wish, Baird."

"But you don't like my staying with Flint?"

"I'm afraid I made clear how I felt about Flint."

Henderson's mouth tightened. "Don't be utopian. What could my leaving *Fact* do?"

"Nothing——"

"Of course."

"Except to you, Baird."

The fire crackled. At last Henderson asked, "What arc you going to do?"

"I don't know."

He went to her, took her shoulders, tried to turn her to him. "Darling, I know what you're going to do. You're going to marry me. Now. Tonight. This is——"

Genuine anger showed in the way she twisted away and whirled to face him. "*Must* you be banal?" she flashed.

Henderson's fatigue overwhelmed him suddenly. A spasm of rebellion twisted him.

When she spoke again, her voice was weary. "I think you had better go, Baird. I don't feel like quarreling."

"Neither do I." Henderson hesitated. "I'm sorry as hell, Monica," he said with a desperate sense of futility.

"Thanks."

The curt monosyllable made rebellion flame afresh in him. He turned, got his coat and hat, hesitated at the door, looked back. Monica was still staring into the fire.

Henderson took a step toward her.

She said, "Perhaps Flint will let you edit National Features now, Baird. You've been so successful with the magazine."

Henderson strode out of the apartment, his mouth bitter.

XXIV

THE next day was Tuesday, closing day, and Henderson was at his desk at eight o'clock, grimly fighting fatigue. This was not wholly the fruit of a sleepless night. As the winter had dragged out its interminably trying short days, he had found himself exhausted at the end of each, until a stubborn, unremitting weariness was with him constantly, lying like a dulled silver dollar loosely in the front of his head when he rose in the morning, damming off the cool stream of forgetfulness when he would have slept at night.

Flint burst into Henderson's office toward the middle of the forenoon, his face flushed with anger.

"Cable Malone he's through," Flint said furiously. "Now. Today."

"Why?"

Flint threw a letter to the desk: "There, damn it, that's why."

Henderson picked up the letter. It was written on the letterhead of *Fact's* Berlin bureau and inscribed to Finley Allen. "Facts, facts, facts," he read, after sketching a paragraph of personal common-places. "Brother Flint spent a vehement and uplifting week end with me recently, so you understand my passion, *mon vieux?* Finley, I am willing to bet any small amount of depreciated currency that within twelve months our own worthy vehicle of sweetness and light under Brother Flint's earnest and prayerful guidance will be taking an out-and-out pro-Nazi line."

"I've had my eye on Malone for a long time," Flint said harshly. "Malone doesn't belong with *Fact* any longer."

"No?"

"No! I won't tolerate disloyalty. Fire Malone."

"I won't fire Malone. He's the best man in Germany today."

"You will fire Malone!"

Henderson's tired eyes blazed wrathfully. "I'll recall him for three months, put him on a roving job here in the States, and I'll send him back to Germany at the end of that time. And if you don't like that," harshly, "you can go to hell and bring a new editor back with you."

Flint, his eyes hard and hostile, wheeled and strode out of the room.

Just after twelve his telephone rang. As he had done twenty times that day, Henderson started, felt the instantaneous flush of hope that it might be Monica, waited trembling.

The grilled speaker beside his desk burred. His finger fumbled with the switch. "Yes?"

Lord, his secretary, said, "Ted Keating, Mr. Henderson."

Reaction swept Henderson. He picked up the phone, said, "Yes, Ted." He had sent Keating that morning to cover the trial.

"That change-maker," Keating said rapidly, "the one who saw Rains get on the subway at Kew Gardens——"

"What about him?"

"He's changed his story," Keating said. "He's not certain, now, that it was Rains."

Henderson held the phone for a moment, not speaking.

"The court's adjourned," Keating said. "Want me to get interviews or come on back and do up what I've got?"

"Come on back," Henderson said flatly.

Rains' alibi gone. The waiting prolonged. The pressure tightening while he sat here . . .

He saw Lynch Rains' eyes.

Henderson himself rewrote Keating's story. A gong rang as he hurried down the corridor. He glanced at his watch. It was two-twenty. He crossed the clattering newsroom, its tumult at flood, passed down the line of thrumming teletypes, peering at the copy on each until he came to number ten. Here he bent down and clamped the sheet he carried in place over the story the operator was sending.

"Kill that other and give them this," Henderson commanded.

The man's fingers were beating out a correction on the jerking tape even as Henderson spoke. An instant later the machine at his elbow broke into a startled ding-ding-ding-ding-ding, and the new dispatch was stitching back and forth across the trip-licate Manila sheet under its glass face, while Henderson watched.

From then on, Henderson was too rushed to heed the simmering feelings which the incident had loosed in him.

He was standing at a proofreader's shoulder, behind the triple-glass wall that dammed out the tumult beyond, when from the corner of his eye he caught the infinitesimal signs that showed the end was near. For an instant he felt a shaft of despair, knowing that he could not much longer escape the introspective guilt that he had been resisting all day. His eyes fell to the sheet the youth in the headphones was following word by word with his pencil. It was the trial story which Henderson himself had written.

As he watched, the reader said into his breast-plate mouthpiece, "OK," slashed a check mark across the copy, throwing it aside to go on to the next.

The quintuple gong sounded sharply. The clamor slackened, leaving a pulsing, nerveless vacuum in which men slumped at desks or reached wearily for cigarettes.

Henderson walked toward the corridor. As he passed the Production Manager, drooping on the corner of a desk, clip board in his slack hand, Henderson inquired out of habit, "Book closed, Larry?"

The other nodded. "Last plates on the way."

Back in his office, Henderson ignored the work drifted on his desk.

His sickening suspicion of the night before returned. Impelled by the need for action, spurred by the realization of his defection, he rose, got his hat and coat. With a deliberation in which there was something uncertain and hesitant, he went out of the office, out of the building. When he reached the street he walked rapidly away as if fleeing a threat whose durable essence had suddenly been revealed to him anew.

XXV

AN HOUR after he left the office Henderson stopped his car on the narrow, forest-hung road at the spot where Norton's body had been found. Darkness had long since come. Distantly, across the frozen meadow, he could see lighted windows in the servants' quarters of Flint's Georgian house.

He had, impelled by no clearly traced design, driven from town along the route the murdered publisher had taken that August night. Now he was sitting where Norton had changed a tire, where he had been struck down as he knelt unfastening the lugs, where . . .

Henderson's thinking brought up with a shock as when slowly meshing gears bite into some hard obstruction.

Above the narrow road stretching on before him in the cold brilliance of his lights, the arched trellis of barren boughs was uneasy in a bitter January wind. The rhododendron bushes lining the roadside, pinched and hungry-looking, huddled shivering together. A bareheaded girl on a roan horse cantered surprisingly out of the darkness behind him, looked over her shoulder, and roweled her mount to a gallop; its hoofbeats drummed away down the sandy road, died, and left nothing but the whistle of the wind and the creaking branches overhead.

Henderson looked about him in the reflected twilight of the Cord's headlights, made sure he had chosen the spot aright, and leaned forward to note the mileage on his speedometer. Then he drove away, accelerating rapidly, overtaking the girl on the roan horse just as the narrow road opened out on the highway. He slowed and read the speedometer again as he passed the entrance to the Norton grounds. It was six-tenths of a mile from where he had started. As he passed the gate, he leaned forward to stare into the rushing darkness, visualizing the house of gray fieldstone, empty now, solid, incommunicative, crowning a long, arrogant slope of landscaped lawn, only its shuttered upper story and spaced chimneys showing through the interwoven leafless branches of the elms by day.

Six-tenths of a mile. Twelve city blocks. From Fortieth Street to Fifty-second. For a man of Norton's athletic stride a ten- to twelve-minute walk.

On his return to town, chilled, morose, he had dinner at an out-of-the-way restaurant on Sullivan Street, near the lower edge of Greenwich Village. While he ate, the question which had emerged from the ruck of his indecision wove in and out through his thoughts, a small insistent question, a question too small for a condemned man's life to hang upon it, a question so trivial that no one had thought of it before.

Why had Philip Norton set to changing the tire himself that sultry August night?

Why had Norton undertaken a task so odious to him when, conditioned by his background, he might be expected to demand service in such an emergency—and when service had been available at the end of a ten-minute walk?

Why had Norton . . .

The implications of the question quickened in his fatigue-drugged mind.

There were two possible answers: Norton had not been changing a tire at all; the whole situation had been synthetically set up as an elaborate blind to give the impression of a casual nocturnal encounter. Or, Norton had changed the tire, *but with assistance.*

How had that tire been hurt? Henderson tried vainly to remember whether this had been brought out at the inquest or in the investigation which followed. Slashed? A nail driven into it, perhaps? Some mark which, on examination, would show it had been purposeful? Potter, Norton's chauffeur, might remember, for he must have repaired the injured tube. But Potter had been dismissed months ago. Julia might know where he could find Potter. He signaled a waiter, gave the man a five-dollar bill, and walked out into the damp, chill street, the mist thickening once more in his mind.

He sought to clarify it—by crystallizing it in some clean focus to control and precipitate it—and found himself balked, until inevitably his imagina-

tion coursed back to that August night on Flint's
terrace. In his frustration, it seemed to him that
from that night dated all the confusion and perplex-
ity in his present world. Like a combing divide, that
night struck upward to shut him off from the peace
which lay beyond it, behind him, irretrievably behind him. On that night Norton had been killed, on
that night Flint had laid siege to Monica, on that
night Danisher had disappeared and Lynch Rains
had walked into the latticed shadow of bars, on
that night Julia Norton and Flint's chauffeur . . .

Henderson swerved to the curb abruptly, leaped
out, and went into a drugstore, his eyes smoldering.
Strange how easily he remembered the number she
had given him.

Thirty minutes later he stepped out of an elevator in one of the Waldorf towers and touched a button beside a door. The door opened, and Julia, de-
light rippling in her voice, was saying, "Baird! How
marvelous your calling and coming in like this. I
was about to weep from sheer boredom."

As he entered the room, passing close to her, he
breathed the sharp pungence of the scent she always wore, the scent which had before been subtly
repellent to him. Now he was aware, swiftly, insis-
tently, of the full-bodied, feral urgency thinly con-
cealed beneath its almost metallic sheen.

She closed the door and stood for a moment, her
hand on the knob, color flowing beneath the trans-
lucent bronze of her cheeks, her pointed breasts,
modeled by the silken gold of her fitted house coat,
rising.

She said, "Well?"

Henderson's nostrils moved. "Shall we go somewhere, Julia? I'm at loose ends, too."

She said, "You're a darling," softly, and came toward him, her mouth smiling sullenly, her eyes sultry.

There was a harshness in Henderson's throat as he held her, his hands hot against the sheer stuff of her gown, against her curving back, her soft parted lips seeking his.

When she had gone to dress, wrath flamed in him, wrath and instant fear because he had come to her this way. The fear, however, was less directed outward than inward upon the imperceptible treacherous springs of his own behavior, and to deaden the fear he found himself picturing the nervous, artificial carnality of night clubs he knew.

They returned to the hotel a little after four. Her maid admitted them to the suite, and as they entered, the girl said respectfully, "Mr. Flint called, madame."

Henderson's mind snapped, and he was aware on the instant why he had come. That revelation had an immediately sobering effect. Coolly he contemplated the best way to accomplish what he wanted, helping her off with her wrap, touching the smooth whiteness of her shoulders with his fingertips.

The maid brought glasses, a siphon, and a squat bottle of King's Ransom; then she went to her own room in another part of the hotel. Julia lay back against the cushions of the deep bisque couch, kicked off her gold pumps, and ruffled her hair, yawning at Henderson, who was busy at the tray.

"Come here," she said drowsily.

Henderson measured whiskey deliberately. He asked, "Julia, do you remember the migraine Hugh had the night we were all at his house?"

Her lazily massaging fingers were suddenly still. After a moment she said, "Um."

Henderson held the siphon and looked at her. Suspicion lay already in her sleepy eyes. Henderson, aware that he had bungled by not going to her first, disarming her before he led up to it, knew that it was too late now, and came at once to the crucial question.

"Was the blind up in Hugh's room?"

"What are you driving at?" she asked.

"Do you remember?"

"This is a hell of a time."

"Do you?"

She sighed, moved her shoulders deeper into the soft cushions. "Um."

"Was it open?"

"Unh-hunh. Why?"

Whiskey splashed as Henderson's hand slipped. "I just wondered."

He carried the glasses to the couch, handed her one. She motioned for him to sit beside her. Henderson, looking down, his mouth drooping, shook his head. "Night cap," he said easily. "I'm a working man."

Her eyes opened wide. She said, "That's a lie. You and Hugh never worked on Wednesday in your life."

Henderson sat down. Her hand rose, hesitated. The fingers smoothing his hair were shy. Something in that uncertain touch made him suddenly conscious of the trickery he was practicing on her, and he hated himself.

"By the way, Julia," he said, keeping his voice casual, "I need a chauffeur. I wanted to ask——"

"I'll drive for you," she said lazily. "I'll drive for you anywhere."

He laughed, touched the tip of her nose. "Do you know where Potter is?"

"Um."

"How could I find him, I mean?"

"Baird," she said petulantly, her hand on his head urgent.

He looked at his watch. "I must go, Julia. Really."

"Don't be this way."

"Then tell me."

"Tell you what, darling?"

"How I can find Potter."

She squinted at him, wrinkled her nose. "You're funny."

"I've a passion to get him. I've been trying to trace him," he lied.

"If I tell you——"

"Tell me." The absurdity of the play struck him, and he wanted to laugh. Yet, Potter could tell him . . .

"Through the Mason Agency," she said. "That's how we got him. I don't know—*Baird!*"

He took her hand, kissed it lightly, laid it on the couch, and rose.

"Thanks, my dear. I meant it, Julia. I've a day before me."

Sullenly she watched him put on his coat, ignored his good night.

Just as he closed the door, Henderson heard the glass crash against it.

XXVI

EVEN during the brief hours of uneasy sleep, Henderson's mind circled about one imperative point which Julia's confirmation of the suspicion he had struggled against made suddenly luminous and inescapable. As he showered and dressed next morning, he went over its implications coldly, reflectively.

As soon as he reached the office, he called the Mason Employment Agency, learned that Potter was now employed at an estate near Rye. He put in a call for Potter, and to his astonishment was immediately successful. Potter remembered repairing the tire, yes. The tube had been pinched, and a hole rubbed in it.

So the damage to the tire had been genuine, and Norton's act unposed. That meant—there was no shred of doubt in Henderson's mind now—that Norton had had assistance. Someone riding with him? Someone casually encountered on the road as Norton walked homeward to summon Potter?

Danisher had been in the neighborhood that

night. Danisher had disappeared. Yet only yesterday another letter—the fourth—had come from
Danisher. Addressed to Flint, it had unaccountably
been mixed in Henderson's own mail and opened by
his secretary. Typed, mailed from South Boston, its
tone differed not at all from the three which had
preceded it.

Since it was Wednesday, *Fact's* offices were all
but deserted, only a skeleton clerical staff being on
duty after the climax of Tuesday's closing-day rush.
Henderson went to Flint's secretary.

"Sellars," he asked, "do you have the letters from
Danisher—the ones that have come since he disappeared?"

"They're in the vault, Mr. Henderson. We had
them photostated, though. I can give you a set of
the photostats."

Henderson returned to his own office with the
four stiff photostats, suspicion darting in his mind
now like a caged wasp. He sat down, placed the
carbon paper over a sheet of flimsy, and laid one of
the photostats on the carbon paper. With the blunt
point of a paper knife as stylus he carefully traced
the signature, *George Danisher.*

He put the photostat aside, took another, traced
its signature on another sheet of flimsy. Not until
he had repeated the operation on all four, using a
different flimsy for each, did he lay the paper knife
down. He had spaced the tracings differently, so
that when he assembled the four tissue sheets and
held them to the light, he could bring all the signatures into place by adjusting the overlapping edges
individually.

The result was glaringly apparent at first glance, but Henderson fussed with the papers until not the least doubt could remain.

Save for infinitesimal waverings caused by his cramped fingers, the four signatures showed sharply as one.

A chiseled inscription on a tombstone could have been no more conclusive.

Though he had expected this, the impact left Henderson suddenly numb. Norton had been opposed to the development of *Fact-On-The-Air*. Over Norton's opposition, Flint could never have proceeded with this, his most passionate ambition, this plan on which he was willing to stake everything. *Fact-On-The-Air* was now within a few weeks of completion, and Flint had said . . .

What had Flint said?

Henderson heard the words as clearly as though they were being spoken aloud: *"Here is what Phil and I were planning. You and I are going through with it. We're going to make it a monument to Phil . . ."*

With the memory came a momentary vertigo as if some essential co-ordinate in his personal space had shifted.

Yet what was to be done?

What?

XXVII

ON Friday morning, Henderson, stepping from the elevator into *Fact's* mural-splashed waiting room a little after nine, encountered two telephone linemen, bags and coiled wire slung from their shoulders.

"Trouble?" he asked sharply.

The taller of the two, a gangling, leather-faced youngster, shook his head. "Putting in a line."

Henderson started past them. Then just as the indicator clinked and a downbound car slid open, he turned. "What line?" he demanded.

"Down to the Rains trial," the slim lineman answered, and the elevator closed behind them.

The sharp-faced boy at the information desk said, "I think Mr. Flint ordered it last night, Mr. Henderson."

A moment later Henderson burst into Finley Allen's book-heaped office and seized the Literary Editor's phone. "Get me the office manager."

Finley Allen, to whom a typewriter was the instrument of Beelzebub, looked up from the pad over which his fat fingers were steering an outsize pencil. His mild, magnified eyes were disapproving. "Fine way to muddy up the Pierian Spring," he grumbled.

"Scott," Henderson said sharply, "I hear there was a new line installed this morning. Where—" He listened a moment and jammed the telephone back into its cradle. He stared down at Finley Allen's Buddha-like curiosity. "Hugh's had a direct wire to the Criminal Courts Building put in. Roman Holiday," he said bitterly.

"Why?"

"Are we publishing a scandal sheet with a run every half-hour?" Henderson demanded.

"Where is that wire?" Allen said. "I'd like to keep track, myself."

Henderson looked at him a moment. "In Hugh's office," he said sharply, and went out.

Even the telegram which came from Monica in Albany, asking him to meet her train that evening, failed to cool Henderson's simmering rage. An early edition of the *Telegram*, brought back by his secretary after lunch, caught his eye.

"Prosecution Demands Chair," he read. He picked up the paper, his eyes running down the double-column story.

". . . summing up before the jury, shouted, 'If this man's powerful position causes you to hesitate in imposing the death penalty, you will be contributing to the certain collapse of everything which free Americans hold dear . . .' At this point the prosecutor was warned by the Court to restrict his remarks to the evidence. . . . This man is a Democratyrant, who, masquerading as a legitimate labor leader, would stop at nothing to . . .' "

Henderson's temper shortened as the afternoon wore on, and once, quite contrary to his wont, he flashed out in instant fury at a teletype operator on whose machine he had caught a minor error of phrasing.

"Another mistake like that, and there'll be a new man at this printer," he said furiously, and at once wondered what he himself was doing there, spying on the operator. He walked away, chagrined, and a few minutes later left the offices.

Why did he not act?

He told himself viciously that he was a forceless dawdler. Yet, others—the police, Rains' legal staff, Flint's detectives—these had access to all that he knew. The letters from Danisher had been made public; the open window above Flint's terrace from which the lane was visible its entire length below the sloping meadows; they knew all that he himself knew. After all, what proof was there that Rains had not killed Norton? Explosive passion lay back of the man's square, dark-browed impassivity. Had Henderson not seen that passion burst at Flint? He walked faster.

XXVIII

HE had rationalized himself into a species of resignation by the time he entered Grand Central at eight o'clock to meet Monica's train. Yet the lifting eagerness that should have filled him at the prospect of seeing her again did not come. He thought of how Flint had come between them that other time he had waited here in the great polished room with its distant constellations overhead.

His heart leaped, nonetheless, when he saw her coming toward him, her green *tailleur* a pert anticipation of spring, its pleated skirt swinging to her swift stride, daffodil blouse colorful at her throat, coat negligently over her arm in the warm night. So instantly desirable was she that Henderson's voice jammed as he caught her hands, looking hungrily into her gray-green eyes. But she shook her head when he would have drawn her to him. She disengaged her hands, straightened the heather topcoat over her arm.

He said, "I thought you wanted to see me."

"I did, Baird." She smiled quickly and was serious again. "Come. Where we can talk."

They walked down the long shining passage to the Roosevelt and into the bar where they sat on a red-leather bench near the window, Henderson's bloodshot eyes leaping up angrily at the waiter who came at once for their order.

When they were alone, she said, "Baird, I'm certain Lynch Rains didn't kill Norton."

"Why?" shortly.

"Partly intuition, partly a theory that's so fantastic I'm ashamed of it. But it haunts me."

"Where have you been?" he asked suddenly.

She hesitated, looked up as the waiter returned with their glasses. She said, "Mine's the Tom Collins," when he would have given her whiskey. The man shifted the glasses and went away.

"Do you remember," she asked intensely, "what you told me about Norton and Hugh Flint that night at Flint's, Baird?"

He said, "No," gruffly, his strained nerves twitching as he realized with a shock what she was pointing toward. "What?" he asked, when she did not speak at once.

"You said that they divided control of Fact, Incorporated, between them, and that if Norton objected to one of Flint's schemes—the labor articles by Rains, for instance—he could stop them."

Henderson set his glass down, his throat dry despite the whiskey that had just washed it. "Yes?"

"And you said that it was unlikely Norton had actually ordered the articles stopped, but that . . ."

He looked at her sharply when she hesitated.

"What are you driving at?"

"This." She leaned forward, her eyes hot. "You said—remember—'Hugh might have given in *as a concession of some kind.*' "

"Perhaps I did." Henderson's pulse was quickening, a new anger rising within him.

"Do you know whether Phil Norton favored the gamble of *Fact-On-TheAir?*" she asked, point-blank.

Henderson's hand jerked. He said irritably, "Of course he did."

"You know?"

In spite of himself, Henderson's eyes were drawn to hers.

"You know?" she repeated.

"No." He added slowly, "I don't."

Her expression changed abruptly. "Then you have thought of the same thing?" she challenged.

"I've thought of damned little else for a week," he said bitterly.

She caught his arm. "Norton *was* opposed to the scheme, then?"

"I think he was."

"Why?"

"Clark Malory mentioned it to me at Christmas. I thought then he was making it up."

"But now you're sure he wasn't?"

"Pretty sure," Henderson said. "But it's hearsay evidence."

"But——"

"Do you want to wreck the whole thing?"

"What do you mean?" Monica asked.

"The most you can hope to establish is the motive. That's a very small part. If you tip him off, before you've any other evidence, you'll have him on his guard."

"There *is* other evidence."

"What?"

"Those letters from Danisher," Monica said. "They are forgeries."

Henderson frowned.

"Not half a dozen people know it," she said swiftly. "No one seems to know where the originals are, but the prosecution has a set of photostats, and Molloy on the *Telegram* told me they've proved that the signatures were all traced from one genuine sample. Molloy says only one other *Times* man knows it, and the prosecutor's office hasn't leaked."

Henderson asked dully, "What if they are?"

"Someone wrote those letters as a blind."

"It could have been a blind for Rains."

She drew back. After a moment she said, "You don't believe that?"

"Why not?"

"What reason would Rains have had for killing Phil Norton?"

"You heard what he said on the air that night."

Her hand jerked angrily. "That wasn't the speech of a murderer."

"It was the speech of a passionate man—a man who hated Norton," Henderson said.

She started to speak, checked herself sharply.

They did not talk of the murder again, nor did they mention Rains' trial. Only when they were in a cab on the way to her apartment did Monica say suddenly, "You asked me where I've been. I've been trying to trace those letters, Baird. I had Molloy make me a list of the places and dates they had been mailed. All of those places are within three hundred miles of New York." She hesitated. *"And none of them was mailed when Flint was abroad."*

Because this openly voiced suspicion rasped into sharp teeth his own sense of futility, Henderson said roughly, "Don't be ridiculous."

He left her at the door and went home, his eyes burning, the pulsing ache in his head an endless rebuke.

XXIX

AGAIN he slept but a feverish four hours, and got up at last, unrelaxed, the taste of sleeplessness dry and bitter in his mouth, his eyes red, his hand unsteady as he poured himself a drink.

Drawn by a fascination he could not resist, he went, after a hurried, unpalatable breakfast, to the vicinity of the Criminal Courts Building, saw the extra details of police keeping traffic and passersby moving, watched knots of men gather here and there to be dispersed and fall back to clot again at another corner. Silent men, for the most part, men with angry eyes and hard jaws.

A pressman in a white paper cap and ink-stained apron stepped out of a nearby printing shop and stood beside Henderson, watching.

"Ain't that a crime?" the pressman asked bitterly.

Henderson looked at him. "What?"

"Railroading Lynch Rains to the chair."

"Why railroading?" Henderson asked sharply.

The other, who had spoken unconsciously, looked at Henderson critically, took in his expensive brown tweed, his De Pinna tie, his Phi Beta Kappa key. "What kind of a name you got for it?" he asked.

Several men, moving slowly along the sidewalk, stopped, surrounded them, listening.

"If you think the trial's dishonest, why don't you go and tell the Court?" Henderson demanded.

"Wise guy!" someone behind him taunted.

Henderson swung on the critic, a short, bowlegged Irishman with red hair and fierce eyes.

"Sure, whyn't you go an' tell the Court?" the Irishman parroted.

"They're framing him," another said hotly.

Others, drifting along the street, stopped and surrounded them. The little Celt, emboldened by the gallery, stepped toward Henderson. "Say Lynch Rains killed that guy," he challenged shrilly. "Say it, once. Come on. Say it."

"Move on," a voice said roughly. Two policemen shouldered into the group. It broke up, the men straggling down the street. The pressman in the paper cap went back into his shop.

One of the patrolmen nodded at Henderson, who had not moved. He said amiably, "God-amighty, you'd think they was burning him already, wouldn't you?" and walked on past, swinging his nightstick.

When he arrived later at the office, his secretary followed him into the inner room. Henderson dropped down at the desk, gritted his teeth, and stared at the man. "Well, what?"

"Three men from the promotion staff were in a little while ago, Mr. Henderson. They demanded to see you."

Henderson frowned and blinked his hot eyes. "They what?"

"They demanded to see you."

"Demanded to—? What about?"

"I really don't know, Mr. Henderson."

Henderson's mouth tightened. "Call them in."

A moment after Lord had gone out of the room, the dictograph at the side of Henderson's desk spoke. "Mrs. Norton is on the wire, Mr. Henderson."

He picked up the phone, said sharply, "Yes, Julia . . . Oh, Mrs. Norton, I'm sorry. I thought it was Julia . . . No, I'm sorry, I won't have time today, Mrs. Norton . . . Monday? Perhaps. May I call you . . . Very well."

The door opened as he replaced the phone. The leader of the delegation, Cook, was nervous, middle-aged, with furrows about his mouth and sharp nose. The other two, Weller and Houston, lads not long out of college, entered Henderson's office behind Cook and looked serious.

"What is it, Cook?" Henderson motioned to chairs, but the trio remained standing. Immediately conscious of the metallic brusqueness of his question, he was embarrassed.

"It's the two men who were fired Thursday. You discriminated against them."

Henderson frowned. "Discriminated? I don't even know who were let go, Cook. They were the last to be hired, weren't they?"

"Like hell, they were."

"No, Mr. Henderson," Weller answered firmly. "I was the last one to be hired in the department.

There were two more ahead of me in seniority before—"

"Then there must be some mistake," Henderson
interrupted, anxious to be rid of the truculent
Cook. "I told the auditor that where there had to be
dismissals seniority was to be——"

"Like hell you did," Cook broke in angrily. "You
ordered those two fired, Henderson, and you know
damn well you did. You're going to take them back
or else——"

"Or what?" Henderson snapped.

"Or *Fact* won't publish a page until you do."

Henderson, his head throbbing, rose and walked
toward Cook. The other, mistaking his intent, stiffened, clenched his fists.

"You're threatening a strike, Cook?"

"If you don't take those two back, we are, yes."

Out of the pause, Houston said, "One of them
was supporting a blind brother, Mr. Henderson."

"Why does anybody have to be fired?" Weller
asked.

Henderson said slowly, enunciating the words as
a man in the first stages of drunkenness might,
"Because the budget in the promotion department
is inflated, Weller. That is why."

"Did we inflate it?" Cook demanded.

"No, Cook."

"But we have to take the rap for your mistakes?
Is that it, Henderson?"

"I can't see that anyone is taking——"

"Being fired out on your tail when there aren't
any jobs to be——"

"I suppose that is my fault, too, Cook?"

"It's the fault of men like you," Cook shouted. "How much've you cut your own salary? How much has Flint cut his take? Not a cent. But because these two men are fighting for a living wage and decent hours and they've got guts enough to come out in the open and fight, you have to crucify them like any filthy exploit——"

The room reeled. Until he had struck, until he was cupping the sharp pain of his knuckles in his other palm wonderingly, Henderson was unconscious of what had happened in the second that the fog closed down.

Then, for a brilliant lucid instant, he saw Cook on the floor at his feet, saw the blood trickling from the man's mouth, the look that was not anger or hurt or hate, but only a blank, patient surprise.

When Weller and Houston had helped Cook to his feet and the three had left, Henderson sat at his desk, touching his aching knuckles, trying to think . . . trying to remember . . .

With an effort like that of a man in a dream who must throw off a vast weight before he can move his limbs, he regarded the telephone for a long time. At last he found the instrument in his hand. "Tell Mr. Wheelwright I want to see him," he said thickly.

When he saw that he was still holding the telephone, he made his hand replace it, and Arthur Wheelwright, the auditor, was standing in the door.

Henderson leaned forward on his desk, steadying himself with his elbows. "Arthur," he said slowly, "the two men in the promotion department, they—" *(They what? They what?)*

"They what?"

"They were—fired, Arthur."

"Yes," shortly.

(Did Wheelwright see how drunk he was? But he was not drunk, for he always got sick when he was drunk. Sick . . .There, the nausea was coming . . .)

"Why were they—fired—Arthur?" *(He would be sick now when Wheelwright answered.)*

"Hugh sent up word," sharply.

(But he must not be sick until he had said . . .)

"They are to be rehired, Arthur. They are to be rehired they are tobe rehired theyaretobe . . ."

(There—and there—and there—and . . .)

XXX

IT was dusk when he awoke, but whether the dusk of night or morning he did not know. As wakefulness came reluctantly, he rose at last and stumbled across the room to his desk and turned on the light. His fingers tugged at the collar which was constricting his throat. He saw that he was dressed, even to shoes. There was stain on his shoes. His hat lay on the floor beside the bed. Henderson stared at the hat for a long time. Then his eyes moved to the clock by the telephone, where through a slot there showed an abstract day and date. Performing a labored inference, he knew that only three hours had passed. It was seven o'clock. He rubbed his cheek and tried to remember. But beyond that final nauseous disgrace when he had staggered retching to his feet and stumbled out into the corridor, nothing precipitated out of the cloudy confusion that should have been memory.

As if the catharsis of that brutal experience were so sweeping that no emotion whatever remained to him, he sat, unmoving, staring at the vapid clock-face until the bell rang.

The sharp impact of the doorbell startled him, made his heart pound grotesquely.

When Henderson opened the door, Flint stood for a moment, anger etched in his narrow face, and then strode into the room. He said, "Haven't you any sense, Baird?"

Henderson walked to the table, picked up a pipe, and began to fill it. The texture of the pouch and the solid granules as his fingers tamped them into the bowl were like familiar markers in a landscape into which he had stumbled by a strange route.

"I've put up with everything I can, Baird," Flint went on, his tone strangled with passion. "This afternoon was the end."

Henderson nodded. "I was going to tell you that myself, Hugh."

"What in God's name got into you?"

"Cook touched off something I didn't know——"

"To hell with Cook. I mean telling Arthur to re-hire those two agitators. Have you gone completely crazy?"

Henderson looked at him steadily. "Not completely." He applied flame to the pipebowl, drew the acrid, clarifying fumes deep into his lungs. He exhaled, looked again at Flint. "I've been going crazy for several months, Hugh. It took an episode like this to prove it to me. I've been going crazy, Hugh, just as you have. Only it stayed closer to the surface in me."

Flint scowled. "What do you mean? Just as I have?"

Henderson hesitated. Tension between them became a field of explosive force. "A whole complex set of forces established the conditions for good editorship at *Fact* years ago," Henderson said slowly. "Because I sensed what those conditions were, I consciously developed a dual personality, became two persons. As one of those persons I worked for you, did a job into whose meaning I did not inquire too closely. As the other person I disassociated myself from *Fact*, stood aside with a sort of pragmatic indifference, criticized you, criticized Phil, criticized *Fact*, criticized myself, of course. But because you and Phil were responsible for *Fact*, that last did not trouble me greatly.

"I called myself a liberal. I was a liberal. I had a colorless vocabulary with which to express what can only be expressed in words slashed with passion—and the one time in my life that I've needed desperately to act I've been helpless.

"To that extent I fell under the spell of *Fact*. But because I could step from one personality to the other when chagrin threatened, I got along fairly well. Then all at once I couldn't step out of Fact any more. My right hand could no longer play with ideas and give me a specious sense of living the life of reason, because I had to use both hands constantly on the machinery of *Fact*.

"The conditions determining the editorship of *Fact* bore down on me so relentlessly that I no longer had an escape. Do you know what those conditions are, Hugh? They are the same conditions as determine a successful hack portraitist: maximum fidelity to flattering features and minimum of independent thought. It is a type of insanity, Hugh;

an insane man believes fervently that the figures and dimensions he secs—in which he sees the facts—are the figures and dimensions that things really have, and that he is telling you about it truthfully. He must believe that or he would suddenly go sane."

"You always were a muddle-headed idealist, Baird." Flint made a flat derisive gesture. "Well, what are you going to do?"

The pipe suddenly trembled as Henderson took it from his lips. "I'm going to know who killed Phil."

Flint's manner changed. He drew a sharp breath. "I know what you think, Baird." He checked himself abruptly, and then continued, "What if it *was* Julia?" He paused, eyed Henderson sharply. "What if it was Julia whom Phil met that night? Can you prove it? Can anyone prove it? Can any good come from confusing matters and——"

"Clearing Rains' name?"

"There is conclusive evidence against Rains," Flint said rapidly. "If there weren't, I'd be the first to demand his release. Rains is a dangerous influence, Baird. Rains is a demagogue. The only way such men can be restrained is by force. As long as any doubt at all remains about his innocence, the ends of a more fundamental justice demand——"

"His death."

Flint hesitated. He stood just beyond the yellow cone of light. Even in the shadows, Henderson could see how the splotches of red deepened in his narrow cheeks. When Flint spoke, his voice was casual, quiet. "Which is the greater injustice, Baird? That one man should die, or that thousands

of men should be driven by his selfishness and hatred and ambition and fanaticism to destroy not
only themselves and their fancied enemies, but the
very order and decency that *is* justice?"

XXXI

THE offices were empty. For that Henderson was grateful. Despite the objective relief he felt to have it settled, he could not escape a certain human chagrin as he opened for the last time the paneled room that had been Norton's and then had been his. But when he had cleared the desktop and winnowed the truck in its drawers, a feeling of incompleteness assailed him. Was there no more than this to show? Could a man live actively and work within a room for six months and leave no more traces of his occupancy than these few trinkets, these scattered scribblings?

He thought of the ranked files outside the door by his secretary's desk. He was unaccustomed to them. It took him time to find the proper keys, and when he had unlocked the cabinets, the profusion of their contents appalled him. Lord, his secretary, would have known at once where to look, what desert stretches to skim over, what dockets to examine, what to ignore.

Exploratively he dipped here and there at first.

His own material was mixed with that of the dead Norton as if realia of two cultures in uneasy sands had lost their ordered cleavage and amicably mingled. Despair seized him at the enormity of picking through the whole mass, inch by inch, drawer after drawer. Yet a determination to leave no loose ends raveling after him when he departed drove him on.

He sat down and began at the first drawer. The bulk throughout was Norton's. Apparently Norton's secretary had been a magpie, for the most obscure and trivial memoranda reposed here pressed between contracts, agreements, and documents whose importance was attested by their heads, by the signatures attached.

He went through, item by item, his memoranda to Flint, reading with unsmiling eyes those which betrayed naïvely his newness and unsureness in the autumn. Some were misfiled, out of chronological order, so that running through them as he was doing gave a curious zigzag effect: "Suggest changing distribution medium in Canada," he had written on September 30. The next sheet, bearing the date December 1, was a copy of a letter to Flint in Bucharest and concerned a spring promotion campaign. The next was headed October 15: "About offset costs . . ." Many of Norton's were mixed in, adding to the sense of time confusion. He came to a series of his own, and in the midst of these, found another of Norton's. Looking at it, some automatic mnemonic machinery clicking within him, he felt a shock, It was dated Wednesday, August 18 . . . Phil had been dead many hours when it was written. But that was quite possible. A secretary, coming in early, had found a rack of dictaphone cylinders filled before Norton left the night before, and had transcribed— But no— Henderson remembered Clark had transcribed the cylinders that Tuesday night. So this accounted for the youth's saying that— So it had been true, after all; here was the proof that it was true: "Must repeat emphatically my dislike of radio scheme. Later, when we've consolidated. The boom won't last. We mean to go on after it collapses. Absolutely refuse to mortgage *Fact* to bankers at this time, that is final." The words were like a ringing bell. They were—*they were his own words*. Almost syllable for syllable. It was like a violent momentary schizophrenia to find them mutely reposing here. So impelling was the sense of split unreality, that not at once did he realize that he held in his hand at last the proof for which he had been searching, that his memorandum established conclusively Norton's opposition to the gigantic scheme into which Flint had plunged at once after the other's death.

But not conclusively.

It must be identified beyond any doubt. Again his eyes leaped to the date. The evening before, they had flown out to Long Island in Flint's amphibian, and in the Chatham Bar, where Flint had invited them, Clark Malory had said he must go back and get out Norton's dictation!

This was how the boy had known. Clark could identify this memorandum, could assert its authenticity beyond any lurking doubt. With the memorandum, a motive would be defined—a motive brilliantly high-lighted, from which, bit by bit, the whole careful fabrication of the rest might be traced.

He signed out in the lobby of the building and walked into the street, to be amazed at its somnolence. He looked at his watch. It was ten minutes after four. He had gone into the building a little after eight the night before.

XXXII

WHEN he had eaten, he sat for a few minutes in the suds-scented cafeteria and watched the rhythmic sweeps of the mop advancing across the white tiles. He would go to Cambridge, stop in on Malory, bring him back to New York if necessary lest there be a slip . . .

His thoughts flew to Monica. He made his way to a phone booth and called her, telling her guardedly of the memorandum, of his mission to Cambridge to get Malory, promised to telephone her as he returned with the boy so that she could meet them.

After he reached the garage, it took a quarter of an hour for a grumbling mechanic to shift the crowded trucks and clear a lane for his car. Then, drawing up in the street, he waited for the man to wheel a handcart across the dewy sidewalk and fill the gasoline tank. Henderson stood by, watching the operation, impatient to be gone.

His casual scrutiny brushed over the Cord's lines, the sleek black cowl and raffish top, the gleaming wire wheels, an absurd affectation in this day of steel——

Henderson frowned, walked toward the car, knelt at the left front wheel, still frowning. One spoke was duller than the others. His fingers explored. That was it. The other spokes were each encased in a gleaming chromium shell, snapped on over original white.

The mechanic, hanging his hose on the handcart's mast, looked at Henderson. He said, "That didn't happen here, Mr. Henderson. I meant to mention it to you when you first brung the car in, but I forgot."

Henderson was not listening. Unconsciously he signed the slip which the man prepared for him. His whirling thoughts fixed again on the wheel with its one unarmored spoke. His eyes flew to the clock. It was a quarter after five. There would be little traffic.

Gravel hissed under his tires as he swung in between the ornamental pillars. Was Flint here? Would Flint see him? But—what matter if Flint did see him now?

Grey would be asleep. Henderson must take care not to arouse Grey's suspicions, lest the man, on his guard, refuse . . . But Grey was not asleep. He was working on the washrack in high boots, water splashing from the hose in his hand and covering the sound of Henderson's approach.

Henderson said, "Hello," above the splatter of the stream.

The chauffeur dropped his hose and wheeled. "Oh, hello, Mr. Henderson. You're here early."

A chill apprehension had been born in Henderson as he walked into the garage. The shock of this made him reckless. "Where is the LaSalle, Grey?" he demanded. "The roadster—the one I borrowed one night last summer?"

"We sold it, Mr. Henderson, just a week——"

"To whom?"

"To some chap driving to California."

Grey, watching the chagrin deepen on Henderson's mouth, asked, "Was there something?"

"I left something in the pocket the day I used it. Didn't remember it until this morning."

Grey said, "Maybe I have it. I cleaned out the pocket just before——"

Henderson seized his arm. "Show me."

The chauffeur took him to a cabinet of drawers at the far end of the garage. He opened a drawer. Henderson's nostrils contracted. His hand dove into the shallow tray amongst the miscellany of odd gloves, cigarette lighters, lipstick . . .

XXXIII

HENDERSON did not return on Monday. It was midafternoon Tuesday before he strode into the building lobby, carrying his attaché case. Monica Leeds, waiting near the directory, hurried toward him.

"Where is Clark?" she demanded.

Henderson took her arm, urged her on toward the elevators. "He should be here. He came down Saturday night."

"Then what have you been doing?"

"Wait."

Henderson, ignoring the greetings of those who waited for a car, took Monica's arm and threaded through to the corridor, hurried her along to the door marked *Flint*.

As he hesitated, with his hand on the knob, she asked, "Can you do it?"

He nodded, threw the door open.

There were a dozen men in the anteroom, waiting in a knot about a typist who wore a headphone with a single earpiece, his noiseless machine rustling under flying fingers. Finley Allen, who held the other receiver at his ear, gazed at them, his mild, magnified eyes widening. Shocked for once out of his accustomed neutrality, he blurted, "My God—you!"

"What are they doing?" Henderson demanded.

Bingham, burly Art Editor, looked up from the sheet jerking back and forth in the speeding typewriter. "Show's over. Judge'll charge the jury in five minutes. They cleared the court. Ted's giving us color."

Clark Malory, his burning eyes on Monica, took a step away from the group. He said, "How do you do, Miss Leeds?"

Sellars, Flint's secretary, said, "I'm sorry, Mr. Henderson, but you can't go in now."

"Why can't we go in?"

"Mrs. Norton has been with Mr. Flint all afternoon. Mrs. Norton, senior, came in a short time ago. They are both with Mr. Flint now."

Henderson's mouth was grim. "Come on, Clark." To Finley Allen, "Tell Ted not to leave that line."

Henderson, ignoring Sellars's protest, opened the door to Flint's inner, soundproofed office. He stood back for Monica and Clark to enter. The boy looked at him sharply, high lights glinting on his polished lenses. "I thought you didn't work here any more, Henderson."

Henderson closed the door behind them. Flint sat at his desk, the angular planes of his narrow face flushed. Julia lounged on a chair arm in a corner of the room, her eyes angry, her red mouth sullen. Across the desk from Flint sat an erect, ener-

getic matron with a Roman nose, a cigarette dan-
gling from a corner of her thin lips, with an air of
astringent disapproval and a Schiapparelli chic that
shamed even Julia.

Flint's eyes leaped alive as Henderson closed the
door.

Mrs. Norton turned, said sharply, "Baird! Where
have you been?"

"I'm sorry I couldn't call you yesterday morning,
Mrs. Norton."

The woman's hawk eyes fastened on Monica.
She said sharply, "You're Monica Leeds," then to
Henderson, "It's time you showed up. I was just
telling Flint——"

"You may go, Clark," Flint interrupted.

Henderson said, "No."

Flint's glance leaped at him again with fresh
hostility.

The boy looked at Flint and then back at Henderson, his burning eyes doubtful. Henderson said
quietly, "I came to tell you, Hugh, that I know who
killed Phil."

Julia slipped from the arm of the chair and took
a step toward them.

Mrs. Norton cried, "What?"

Flint's angular face was emotionless.

"It was not Rains," Henderson went on. "If Rains
were to be electrocuted, two men would have died
because Phil was murdered."

"Two?"

There was movement, a minute stifled movement.

"Rains," Henderson said, "and Danisher."

Again there was the movement, the quick, quenched spasm of a trapped animal.

"Danisher was killed the same night Phil was," Henderson said.

"How do you know?" Mrs. Norton cried. Her handsome face was white.

Henderson opened his attaché case. He took out the photostats, the flimsies bearing the traced signatures, arranged the latter so that their identical lineaments were as one. He showed the tracings to Mrs. Norton and laid them on Flint's desk. Julia, coming quickly, looked over Flint's shoulder.

"The signatures on these letters from Danisher were traced from one genuine copy," Henderson said.

Julia looked up intensely. "That doesn't prove that Danisher——"

"And this," Henderson went on, *"is a specimen from the typewriter on which they were all written."*

He took another sheet of paper from the case as Monica Leeds gasped.

"Let me see that," Flint commanded.

Henderson, with Monica at his elbow, walked to the desk and laid the sheet down. Mrs. Norton rushed to them to peer at the paper through her lorgnette. Flint moved one of the photostats, folded the paper and laid it down line-to-line. The similarity in typing was glaring: the broken serif on the "m," the notched leg of the "h," the angled "l."

"Where did you get this?" Flint demanded.

Julia walked back to the chair and threw herself into it.

"Phil was killed," Henderson said slowly, "in order that you could go on with *Fact-On-The-Air*, in order that he could not veto the expansion you so passionately——"

A hoarse cry from Norton's mother interrupted him. She was staring at Flint.

Flint, catching her eyes, leaped to his feet. His mouth moved twice mutely before he could gasp, "What are you saying?"

"That is true, isn't it, Clark?" Henderson asked.

As the others in the room stared at him, startled, the white-faced boy sank into a chair.

Henderson continued quietly, "You knew that Norton was unalterably opposed to *Fact-On-The-Air*, Clark, because you typed the memorandum that night—the memorandum in which he said so, defiantly. Isn't that right, Clark?"

Monica's hand on Henderson's arm tightened. Flint dropped into his chair. Mrs. Norton, standing beside him, leaned forward on the desk on her clenched hands.

"So you followed Phil out from town, didn't you, Clark? You came on him in the lane and offered to help him change the tire. Phil would never have changed a tire himself; it was quite appropriate for you to help him. You killed him. Danisher was wandering around near there that night. Danisher saw you. You were in a maniacal mood. So you killed Danisher out of——"

"No," the boy cried in a strangled voice. "That's a lie. Danisher attacked—" He checked himself, his eyes terrified.

"He attacked you? Perhaps he did. That doesn't matter. So you put Danisher's body into the car and drove away."

He paused a moment. No one in the tableau moved.

"But as you rushed away, skirting Phil's car widely, you struck a stump—and one of the chromium shields over the wire spokes on your wheel was ripped off. I found it the next afternoon. The rear tire had passed over it, flattened it. I didn't know what it was. I didn't know until day before yesterday. Then I knew what had happened, but I didn't know how to prove it.

"I went to Cambridge. The odds against my finding the typewriter on which you had written the Danisher letters were appalling, but— Well, I found the typewriter this morning, Clark, the old Royal in the back room of your college magazine office. That was incredibly careless of you."

The silence thickened. The boy's eyes moved from Henderson to Flint. His white face tightened. As Flint said nothing, there dawned in Clark's eyes slowly the glint Henderson had seen when Clark leaped at the waiter that night they dined together.

"Will you tell us," Henderson asked, "or must the police——?"

The glint blazed into wildness. Malory, wrenching his gaze from Flint, gave a delirious laugh. "The police! Do you think you can scare me with nonsense like that? The police! What can the police do? What can any of you do?" He broke off, and for an instant as his wild eyes sought Flint's face there was desperate appeal in them. Then it passed.

"I killed Norton," the boy shouted. "Do you hear me, Flint? I killed Norton." He rushed to the desk to bend down and peer at Flint with mad eyes. "None of you could have done that. His wife couldn't. You couldn't. No matter how you longed to, none of you could have done that."

He backed away from Flint. His maddened eyes quieted as they rested on Henderson. "You'll find Danisher with a set of tire chains and a gate around his neck at the bottom of the Sound off Sea Cliff—if you're so damned anxious to find him, Henderson."

As the boy whirled and sped to the door, throwing it open, Flint leaped from his desk and shouted, "Stop him!"

XXXIV

DURING the confusion, Julia slipped out. Henderson missed her when he returned to the office after word had been flashed to *Fact's* reporter at the other end of the open wire that he might rush back to the courtroom and send a scribbled note to the bench, while the newsroom at *Fact* exploded into new activity and the five o'clock closing gong clanged unnoticed in the hubbub.

Monica Leeds sat on the arm of the grief-wracked older woman's chair, her arm about the other's shoulders. Henderson closed the door, walling back the tumult outside. He walked across the quiet room and looked down, his eyes contrite.

He said softly, "It was a foul way to do it. But you were always such a good soldier . . ."

Mrs. Norton's suffering eyes sharpened. Her mouth was a harsh line. She said, "I can still take it, Baird," huskily, and tried to smile. "You used to like me when you were a youngster—for being a good soldier." Her groping hand caught his. He drew her up. She faced him a moment, struggling, and then her face sagged. She wept against his shoulder while he stroked her hair and murmured, "There, there," his own lips unsteady for an instant.

Monica walked to the window to stare out.

At last Mrs. Norton drew back, sniffed, said, "That was a hell of a thing to do," jerked the handkerchief out of his breast pocket, wiped her eyes, and put it back patting it sharply. She said, "I always liked you, Baird," softly. Then her voice sharpened again. "Come here," she called to Monica. "Sit down, you two."

She herself dropped into the chair behind the desk. "Where's Flint?" When Henderson said that Flint had gone home, she snorted, "These strong men." She picked up a paper knife and shook it at Henderson and Monica. "Can you two run *Fact?*" She waved her hand and went on without waiting for a reply. "Listen, I only got wise to this crazy radio scheme of Flint's about three weeks ago. He was doing exactly what Phil knew he would—wringing the golden goose's neck. Another six months, and the way he was throwing money down that funnel, *Fact* would've been broke. I got busy. Flint had forty per cent of the stock; he was voting my forty. There was twenty more scattered around, and in the last three weeks I've picked up eleven of it. So I'm calling the turn. That's what I wanted to see you about, Baird. Will you two do it?" she demanded.

Henderson said, "No, I——"

"We'll do it," Monica Leeds said firmly, "on one condition."

Henderson frowned at her.

Mrs. Norton asked, "What?"

"That an editorial contract is drawn up by lawyers we select—a contract that gives Baird and me absolutely unrestricted control of editorial policy for five years."

Mrs. Norton's eyes flashed. "How about it, Baird?"

"He will," Monica answered. "What do *you* say?"

There was a grim smile on Mrs. Norton's mouth. "I guess you'll do. Call up your legal lights while I go out and have a talk with the auditor."

Monica's eyes were burning when she turned to him after the other woman had gone. "A free hand!" she said.

"A free hand to—?"

"To try to do something we both believe in," she broke in rapidly. "I'm not a starry-eyed dreamer, Baird. It may be a terrible failure, but isn't it worth the gamble?" she pleaded. "*Fact* will go on. Someone must do it. Why not we?" She walked to him, caught his lapels.

Henderson drew a breath, tilted her chin up. "It's worth the gamble," he said. "But I've one condition of my own——"

"That," she interrupted, her gray eyes laughing, "was one of the things I had in mind, Baird darling."

A moment later Henderson threw the door open and tumult engulfed them, the tumult of a closing day which was at once—fervently he made himself believe this—a closing and a beginning.

The End

TO THE READER

If you enjoyed this book, you will be glad to know that there are many others just as well written, just as interesting, to be had in the Fiction House Press Library.

You will find the Fiction House Press Library online at

www.FictionHousePress.com

www.ingramcontent.com/pod-product-compliance
Lightning Source LLC
Chambersburg PA
CBHW060401030726
47497CB00003B/809